OPERATION
THUNDERBIRD

OPERATION THUNDERBIRD

RED RAIN #6

RACHEL NEWHOUSE

To Jon

because you
never gave up on me
even when
I lost my way

JULY 2076

1

Punching my boyfriend in the face was not my idea of a fun date.

"Pull back, regroup, try again," my uncle Tower called from outside the ring.

We both obeyed. I slid a few feet back from Stanyard, my bare feet dragging on the padded canvas floor. We were in the gym on the lower level of the base, where we'd been spending most of our afternoons for the past several weeks. Every day we came down here to train, and every day I ended up on the ground, gasping for breath.

Today, clearly, would be no exception. Even though we were several floors beneath the ground, the cold air did nothing to stop me from sweating profusely.

"You good?" Stanyard asked, pushing his tousled dark hair off his forehead. We'd been going for half an hour already, but he barely looked winded. Probably because I hadn't given him much of a fight.

"Yeah," I lied, and wiped the sides of my face with both hands. I'm sure I looked anything but cute with my tangled blonde hair and smudged eyeliner. Why I'd bothered to put on makeup this morning was beyond me, but something about knowing Stanyard would be picking me up made me want to break out the blush and bronzer.

The frown returned to his dark eyes, but he didn't argue. "Ready?"

I nodded, not trusting my voice.

"On the count of three." Tower leaned both hands on the rope railing. "And let's try to act like you mean it this time."

My heart returned to its second home in my throat. *Please don't.*

"One… two… three."

Stanyard lunged forward and grabbed my wrist. I struggled to remember the motions even as his touch ignited a flurry in my stomach. I should have been feeling fear, adrenaline, the fight to survive. None of those could have been further from my mind.

It's not real, I coached myself as I yanked my arm back, using his momentum to pull him forward. I hit his chin with the palm of my hand—harder than I intended. I heard his teeth click and winced.

No one's getting hurt. I forced myself to grab his shoulder and shove him down. *This is just practice.* I pretended to kick him, knocking his chest with my knee. He grunted. *And he's not your boyfriend.*

But even as I pushed off him and darted away, I realized I didn't believe any of those statements.

"Good one," Stanyard coughed. He straightened and turned to face me.

I scanned his face, searching for bruises. "You okay?"

He wiped his chin on the back of his hand, his grin returning. "Never better."

Tower was not impressed. "You need to be faster, Philadelphia. Again."

Stanyard nodded at me, and we repeated the motions with what *I* thought was an increase in efficiency. I looked to my uncle for approval.

He shook his head. "Again."

I was really starting to hate that word.

Tower paced around the ring as Stanyard and I continued our morbid dance. "This isn't for show. A real attacker isn't going to be sluggish."

A real attacker also wouldn't be staring at me with a secret half-smile, one eyebrow raised in a gesture only I could interpret. I glared at Stanyard as I clipped him in the chin, wishing I could wipe the feelings right off his face and off my heart.

Tower had similar thoughts. "Stanyard, stop flirting. Pretend like you actually intend to hurt her."

The light went out of Stanyard's eyes, and I swallowed.

"And you," Tower pointed a scarred finger at me, "I want you to forget his face. Pretend it's not him. Pretend it's someone who actually hurt you—you have plenty of options."

He wasn't wrong, but no matter how hard I tried to conjure Carnegie, or Ambrose, or Thames, I couldn't superimpose a nightmare over Stanyard's face. I couldn't erase the kind words, the gifts, the *prayers* he had showered on me for the past month. I couldn't imagine him as an enemy, not anymore.

He grasped my wrist and yanked me forward, but instead of reacting, I just froze, all my complicated emotions icing over. I stumbled and crashed into him. He dropped my hand and caught me—like he always did.

He chuckled and set me on my feet. "Easy there."

Tower sighed and rubbed his temples, clearly wondering how his illustrious military career had brought him to this point.

"Sorry," I mumbled to literally no one, quickly stepping back. "I just wasn't paying attention."

"And now you're dead."

I stifled a groan as Jayde walked into the room. He was the commander of the base, and he was the one person I didn't want to watch me train. Probably because he was the one making me do it.

He grasped the railing and swung his muscular body into the ring. "If that happens on the street, you're done."

I rubbed my sore arm. "I'm trying."

He wasn't appeased by the sacrifice. "That's not good enough. You should be better than this by now."

His words stung like a slap across the face—because he was right. I should be better than this by now.

"Lay off her," Stanyard grunted.

"Why should I? No one else will." Jayde's combat boots sunk into the padding as he strode towards me, and I registered what was happening—a second too late. He grabbed my hair and yanked my head back.

I yelled as my mind blacked out in panic. *What do I do, what do I do?* I should know what to do; we'd rehearsed this. I struggled to recall the right move, but all I could see were flashing colors. I scrabbled at his arm, my sweaty fingers slipping off his thick wrist.

Jayde let me struggle. "Ambrose didn't lay off her. Carnegie didn't lay off her."

Stanyard shouted an objection, but Jayde blocked him with his arm. "Nic didn't lay off her."

Rage replaced the fear in my lungs. "Don't talk about Nic like that!"

Jayde's fingernails dug into my scalp as he gave me one last yank and let me go. I slipped on the floor and fell. The impact shuddered through my joints and threatened to knock tears loose.

Stanyard dropped down next to me. "Phil."

"Don't help her," Jayde snapped. "She gets up on her own, or not at all."

"Don't be a jerk," Tower called, but less kindly.

Jayde folded his arms over his chest. "If she wants to lead us, she has to train like us. My men won't follow a 'Blue Fire' who can't pick herself up." He spat my callsign like a threat, and I took it as one. He leered over me. "Get up."

Stanyard touched my arm, but I shrugged him off. I was weak, but I was not a failure. Even if I could do nothing else, I could always get up again. I'd proven that to Ambrose, Carnegie, even Nic. I would prove it to Jayde, even if it broke every bone in my body.

I am Blue Fire.

I planted both palms on the mat. With a breath and a prayer, I pushed myself up and turned to face Jayde. I slid one foot back, put both fists up, and stared him down. "Again."

He grunted, approval flashing across his green eyes. "All right then, show me what you've learned. Try to punch me." He copied my stance and crossed his arms defensively in front of his face.

I quelled a spasm of anxiety. *I can do this.* At least punching Jayde required less imagination.

Stanyard gave us a wide berth. I swung my right fist at Jayde, and he ducked. I followed with my left first and then my right again. He continued to roll, motion effortless.

"Focus," Tower coached from somewhere behind me.

I lunged, overcompensating. Jayde easily sidestepped, and I stumbled forward, nearly ending up on my face.

Jayde pulled back and waited for me to gather my wits. "Operation Blue Fire launches in three months," he said, not sounding the least bit winded. "These people are going to expect a warrior, not a victim."

I am not a victim. We squared up again, and I threw another punch, more purposeful this time. I had been a victim before, but never again. I chose this. No one was forcing me to be Blue Fire. I chose to join the rebellion because I believed it could be done. Because it was the right thing to do.

"We're asking them to risk their lives to stand up to the government." Jayde raised his arm and clipped my next strike out of the air. "They're going to expect you to do the same."

I swung again, not caring that I hit his arm—at least I was hitting something. I had already risked my life several times to resist the United, and this wouldn't be my last. Only this time, my rebellion would look a little different. This time, I wouldn't be blowing up a lab or destroying a weapons factory. I wouldn't be recording a video in an empty room, begging someone, anyone, to help. I wouldn't be fighting alone.

No, this time, I would be leading an army.

"We only get one shot at this. We have one chance to pull the trigger, and if we don't move the needle, the United will finish us off." Jayde deflected my next shot, then lowered his arm to give me another chance.

I took the window of opportunity, pausing to measure my movements. I focused on pivoting my foot and putting my hip into it, just like Tower had taught me. Jayde was right—we wouldn't get another chance. There were no do-overs with Operation Blue Fire. On the chosen day, I would go on air and tell everyone it was time to fight. At my signal, citizens across the globe—anyone who followed the thunderbird symbol—would stand up and say no. They would burn factories, go on strike from their government jobs, destroy paperwork—whatever it took to show the United that we would not conform anymore. The unassimilated were going to resist, and we were going to do it together.

There was no going back from that. Either Operation Blue Fire would succeed, and the government would lose its grip on society. Or it would fail, and we'd all be branded as criminals. Anyone who spoke out would be executed, and my people—Christians and other dissidents who refused to sign the file—would suffer in containment camps until the government decided to wipe us out.

Operation Blue Fire was a one-shot chance at freedom. And its success all came down to me.

I took a deep breath and focused all my muscles into coordinating the next punch. I missed, but not by much—my knuckles grazed his ear as he dodged.

He cracked his neck and straightened. "Better, but too slow. Stop reacting. You have to lead. Everyone's looking at you."

His words made my stomach clench with anxiety, and my next swing missed by a large margin. He snorted derisively.

Stanyard shifted in my peripheral. "C'mon, Phil." His tone suggested that if I didn't land a punch, he would.

I took a deep breath and closed my eyes. Everyone *was* looking at me whether I liked it or not. I hadn't wanted to be famous, and certainly not for insurrection. I hadn't intended to start a war when I blew up the factory on Rott. All I wanted to do was keep Red Rain, the apocalyptic chemical weapon my father had created, out of the hands of the government.

I'd done that, but now my story was convincing other people to join the fight. Jayde and his allies had blasted my videos all over the internet and made me the face of a rebellion. I was Blue Fire, the thunderbird. I was the one they were listening to. I was the one they trusted.

And now it was my job to lead Operation Blue Fire.

There were days I still doubted. Every time I went live, I stared at the angry red recording light and wondered if someone, anyone, would be better than me. Someone with more experience. Someone with more strength. Someone who hadn't stumbled into this by accident and almost killed her father in the process.

But mistake or not, I was here. I had been chosen—God had chosen me. Only He could have strung all the tragic pieces of my life together and turned them into something worth fighting for. Now it was up to me to finish the job.

I opened my eyes and focused on Jayde's face, tracing an invisible line through the air to his chin. I ground the balls of my feet into the padded floor, tracing the flow of power up my spine and into my arm. Shoving all other thoughts out of my head, I swung my fist with a lifetime of righteous indignation—and landed.

My knuckles cracked into his chin, and I gasped in surprise. The shock rippled up my arm with a burst of elation. *You can do this. You can be one of them.*

Stanyard made a noise of admiration, and I savored it a beat too long. Jayde popped his jaw and swung his foot, knocking my legs out from under me. I collapsed on the ground with a grunt.

"Seriously, dude?" Tower griped. "She got you fair and square."

"Yes, she did," Jayde consented. "And she'll do it again. Get up." He nudged my foot with his boot.

I groaned and struggled to obey. Fatigue seized my joints, reminding me that I'd been training for an hour already. I braced myself against the rope railing. "I need a minute."

I'll never know if Jayde would have relented, because a slamming door and pounding footsteps answered for him. I turned to see my older brother Ephesus jogging towards us.

I smiled at him, feeling a rush of involuntary comfort. His arm cast and nose splint were gone, and his dark brown hair was growing back in. He looked like my brother again, and the sight of him reminded me that there were a few things that hadn't changed over the past few months.

Unlike me. I could never go back to the long-haired, brown-eyed girl he used to know. Some people still called me Philadelphia Smyrna when they thought the government wasn't listening, but to everyone else, I was Andromeda Nolan. Even to my family.

He stopped and tried to return my smile, but I could tell the gesture was harried, nervous. "It's time."

My happiness faded when I remembered why I'd agreed to train this afternoon. Why I was in the basement punching things—so I could forget what was going on upstairs.

Ephesus gulped a breath. "We need you." The statement was directed at me, but he cast a glance at our uncle. "They're ready to bring Dad online."

2

"Online" was an accurate term, seeing as my dad was more machine than man.

He lay entombed in an incubator, looking like Snow White in her glass coffin. His newly regenerated skin was almost as pale as hers, and there were patches and wires connected to almost every square inch of his body. A tangle of tubes snaked from the incubator and tethered him to the half a dozen machines that were keeping him alive. Everything whirred and beeped and gave conflicting readouts, making the whole room twitch and vibrate like an old man having a seizure.

It was only a slight improvement over the block of solid cryoprotectant he had been encased in a few weeks before.

Today, a new monitor had been added to the chaos. It sat on a stand at eye-level, with a curved screen over four feet wide. On its display trilled an endless scroll of green code.

Andes, the Scotsman I'd hired to oversee my dad's revival, stood in front of it, his thick fingers flying over the screen with a surprising amount of dexterity. "You got me wired in yet, lad? I'm still not seeing any input."

There was a thud and an exclamation muttered in Russian from behind Dad's machine. Another grunt, and then Lev appeared, a wad of wires in his hands. "Try that."

The code on the display flickered and rebooted. Andes clapped his hands together, his tattooed arms bulging. "We're in!"

Lev navigated his lanky body around the tangle of machines. He stopped next to me and saluted, as he did every time we met.

I managed a smile for him. Lev, like me, had lost everything for refusing to assimilate. Only, unlike me, there was no hope that Lev's family could be revived. The United had been less patient with the Jews.

Lev returned the smile and saw himself out, nodding at Tower as he passed. My uncle took up station at the door, guarding the room in watchful silence, like he always did.

Ephesus brushed past me and joined Andes at the monitor. "Are we ready, Cynthia?"

His question was directed at Mrs. Nolan. She stood on the other side of Dad's machine, fiddling with an IV dispenser. "Give me a minute to stabilize his blood pressure."

The sight of the clear liquid flowing down the tube and into Dad's chest made me shudder. "Is he okay?" I asked, too loudly.

She glanced up at me. "He's fine. He's just recovering from the lung transplant, that's all."

I nodded and swallowed, trying to push the fear and guilt back down into my stomach. Mrs. Nolan's tone was guarded, but I knew she wasn't lying to me. We'd moved past that stage, although I don't think either of us knew how to classify our relationship anymore. To the government, she was my adoptive mother. And although she would never be a parent to me, seeing how she had put her nursing skills to use caring for my dad had proven that she at least wasn't an enemy.

"He's done remarkably well for how much freezing damage he suffered." She turned back to the incubator and navigated controls with swift hands. "His body accepted all the transplants and seems to be assimilating them well. The question is if his brain can support them." She looked up at Ephesus.

"That's what we're going to find out. Ready?" He deferred to Andes.

"I don't think I'm the one you should be asking." Andes glanced back, and the burden shifted, as always, to me.

I walked over to Dad's machine. Laying my hand on the glass, I closed my eyes and prayed. My pleas for mercy and healing battered against an impossible wall of *what-ifs*, but I shoved through them all to reach the only One who could save my dad.

Please, God, let him still be in there.

I looked up and nodded at Andes.

He reciprocated the nod and swiped a hand across the monitor. "Right now we've got an implant suppressing his brain function so that the machines can do the living for him. I'm going to release the hold on each organ one at a time so we can make sure he remembers how to breathe."

Ephesus picked up a tablet and keyed instructions onto the screen. "I'm monitoring the electrical readouts."

"And I'm watching his bios," Mrs. Nolan said, squaring herself in front of Dad's incubator.

"One heart, coming online." Andes tapped the screen, and a flicker of electricity arced from the pads on Dad's chest. He convulsed, his legs and arms smacking into the glass.

I tried to scream and gagged on the sound.

"It's okay, it's okay." Mrs. Nolan stuck her gloved hands into the machine and gently laid him back down. "It was involuntary."

I scanned Andes's monitor, as if I had any idea what I was looking at. He navigated menus, his fingers barely lifting from the screen. "I need more power. I'm getting a reading, but it's too weak."

"Coming now." Ephesus typed on the tablet, and another flash of electricity danced across Dad's body. This time, he only twitched slightly, and a new readout blinked to life on Andes's screen. A thin line danced across the corner.

At first, it barely flickered. But then, slowly, it gained strength, the line tracing sharp mountain peaks across the screen. After a few erratic flutters, it settled into a rhythm.

Dad's heart was beating.

Andes cheered and clapped Ephesus on the back. My brother braced himself against the monitor, mouthing prayers of thanks.

Mrs. Nolan donned a wireless stethoscope and laid the receiver on Dad's chest. She listened for several seconds, her eyes on her watch. Then she popped the earpiece out and handed it to me.

I cupped it to my ear with both hands. Dad's heartbeat thrummed, loud and steady.

Warm tears slid down my face. *Thank you, Jesus.*

Tower echoed the sentiment in Latin.

Mrs. Nolan ran several more tests, then Andes took Dad's heart offline again, letting the machine take over so they could focus on another part of his body. The process went on for two hours. There were some scares—his oxygen level wasn't high enough, and his blood pressure was all over the map—but Mrs. Nolan said all those problems were fixable. My dad was going to live.

I repeated those words under my breath until I almost believed them.

While the others worked, I sat in a chair next to Dad's machine and prayed. Stanyard ran in and out, fetching whatever Mrs. Nolan or Ephesus requested.

"Do you need anything?" he asked me when Andes paused the process so everyone could take a break.

"No," I said, not stopping to consider the question.

"Wrong answer," he grunted, and pressed a water bottle into my hands. I stared at the clear plastic for a minute before turning to look up at him.

He smiled.

"All right, time for the big test." Andes strode back into the room, adjusting his ponytail.

I grabbed Stanyard's hand. "Stay. Please."

His fingers held mine, his grip strong and steady. "Always."

Ephesus returned to his post next to Andes. "How are we doing this?"

Andes's fingers resumed their one-man waltz across the screen. "A friend of mine designed a synaptic program that will rapid-fire neural stimuli directly into the cerebral cortex. The computer will read and analyze the electrical responses and give us a good idea of how well he remembers common objects and basic language skills. Should take about ten minutes."

Ten minutes. Ten minutes to have the answer I'd spent weeks praying for. Ten minutes to determine whether my dad was truly alive or dead.

I watched as Mrs. Nolan reached into the machine and gingerly lifted Dad's head. She carefully straightened the wires protruding from the base of his neck.

Andes grunted in satisfaction. "Here we go." Then, without waiting for permission, he launched the program.

The motherboard kicked into high gear, its circuits laboring so loudly I could hear it over the other machines. Code flew across the screen at a pace too fast to humanly read.

The results started tallying in the corner of the monitor. At first, there was a series of comforting green checkboxes. One after another, my father's brain passed the tests.

Ephesus smiled. I leaned forward, my grip crushing Stanyard's hand, as I felt the praises rise on my tongue.

And then there was a red *X.*

And another.

And another.

The monitor made no sound, but my mind supplied the screech of denial I had tried so hard to forget.

Access denied.

The X's continued to pile up until they drowned out the green checkboxes. I closed my eyes, unwilling to stare at the sea of red.

Abruptly, the machine silenced, bringing an unwelcome stillness back into the room. Andes sighed.

"What's the damage?" Ephesus said, voice dampened to keep the emotion out of it.

"He's got some basic object recognition." If Andes was trying to be optimistic, his tone was having the opposite effect. "I'd say we're looking at about a first-grade language level."

Tower made the sign of the cross.

Oh God, my spirit cried, but the only sound my lips made was a moan. Thirty years of experience and two PhDs, gone in a moment. All of my father's expert intelligence wiped from his mind like a whiteboard being erased.

I pulled my hand from Stanyard's to hide my face. He found my shoulder instead.

Ephesus muttered a prayer. "What about his memory?"

"That's the next test."

I dared to look up and saw Andes pull a flash drive from his pocket. "Now we'll run a program of stimuli curated from his life specifically. Memories are stored in a different part of the brain— it's possible for him to lose language skills while still retaining memories."

I straightened. "How common is that?"

"It's not." He glanced back at me with a glare not intended to be cruel. "I warned you, lass."

I sank back in the chair.

Andes plugged the drive into the machine and loaded the program. "Ready?" he asked. Mercifully, the question was directed at Ephesus; I wouldn't have had the courage to answer.

Ephesus sighed and tapped the screen.

The computer whirred. Immediately, red X's appeared in the corner of the screen.

I wanted to look away. I *needed* to look away. But I couldn't. As the marks continued to pile up, the screen filling with blood, I couldn't turn my head. It was as if fingers of ice were gripping my face, forcing me to keep my eyes open as my worst nightmare became reality.

As if thriving off our misery, the program took an eternity to run. No one moved as the computer continued to sign off on Dad's death warrant. And then, finally, it stopped.

Not a single green checkmark was found. My father didn't remember anything. Not even me.

Ephesus stood there, his arms gripping his chest as tears ran silently down his face. I couldn't find the strength to cry. I couldn't find the strength to do anything. I didn't move, or breathe, or speak, or pray. Stanyard's fingers dug into my shoulder, but I barely felt them. Tower stared straight ahead, his glazed eyes drained of any emotion.

"I'm sorry, lass," Andes whispered, his voice suffocated by the heaviness in the room.

I stood up, my limbs feeling like they were treading water. I leaned over the incubator and stared at Dad, the reflection of my face on the glass hovering like a ghost over his sleeping features. I studied the nose and cheekbones that so matched my own and tried to accept the truth I'd spent the last month denying.

My dad was never coming back.

3

"I'm sorry it's late."

I glanced at the dashboard clock in Stanyard's car. It was 5:17. According to the Vons, my host family, that was *catastrophically* late when I was supposed to be home at five. I was somewhat surprised Mrs. Von wasn't pacing the sidewalk, seething.

"It's not your fault," I told Stanyard.

It really wasn't; I'd been trapped in the world's worst family meeting all afternoon. There had been no time to waste on grief. As soon as Ephesus recovered and stuffed his feelings back down where they came from, we immediately started planning what to do with Dad. Mrs. Nolan wanted to run more tests before we woke him up; Andes wanted to order a brain implant that might help supplement Dad's vocabulary. On top of that, Dad would need physical therapy, more cosmetic surgery, and round-the-clock supervision until he adjusted. There were therapists to contact, bills to pay, living arrangements to settle—all the planning and logistics for a reality I didn't even want to live in.

Andes had made a valiant attempt to console me. "His memories may still be in there, lass. He just can't access them because the neural pathways are damaged."

"Can they be repaired?" I looked up at him, trying to decide why he was telling me this.

His eyes wandered, which told me all I needed to know. "They've experimented with it. It hasn't been successful, but… maybe one day."

One day. I didn't dare attach any hope to that statement.

By the time Andes left, it was too late to get me home on time. I didn't care. I had bigger problems than keeping Mrs. Von's universe in balance.

"Do you want me to come in with you?" Stanyard asked.

"No," I sighed. That wasn't exactly the truth, but it wasn't a lie either.

He didn't object. "Call me if you need anything."

"I will," I said, and looked into his eyes so he would know I was being sincere.

I let myself in the back door with my key. No sooner had I shed my shoes than an imposing voice scolded me from behind.

"You're grounded."

I sighed. I'd been praying that the Vons would have a bad memory day and not notice I was gone, but no such luck. I looked up to see Mrs. Von glaring at me, her feet apart so she could fill as much of the hallway as possible.

I put my hands up in surrender. "I'm sorry, I—"

She didn't even give me a chance. "Where have you been? You're," she glanced at her watch, "twenty-one minutes late. You have some explaining to do, young lady."

I had absolutely no intention of explaining the real reason I was late, but I was too tired to come up with a believable excuse. I just stared at her, struggling not to cry. *I can't do this tonight.*

She stopped when she saw my face. "Andromeda? What's wrong?"

What's wrong? I just found out my dad is going to end up exactly like you.

Roseanne and Paul Von Nieuwenhuyse had also lost their minds, although they were the victims of a botched neurosurgery, a failed government attempt to beat the noncompliance out of them. It had taken years of therapy before they were able to take care of themselves again. Despite all their progress, their memories still had the stability of a house of cards, and even the slightest deviation from the pattern—like me being five minutes late—broke them. The only reason Mrs. Von even remembered my name was because I had been home at precisely five o'clock every evening for the past month to repeat it to her. Even now, she looked at me with eyes that were permanently veiled with a shroud of confusion, like she was second-guessing everything she thought she knew about me.

Suddenly, I understood why it was so easy for their daughter Cea to just walk away and pretend they didn't exist.

I'd given Cea a hard time for it once, swore up and down that I'd never give up on my family. But now that my own father had been stripped of his identity, reduced to a shell of a man with no ability to care for himself, I understood why it was so tempting to claim he was dead.

Because, in a way, he was.

"Andromeda?" Mrs. Von tried again. "What happened?"

"I just… got some bad news about a friend who's in the hospital, that's all," I managed. But even as the words "that's all" left my lips, I realized that *wasn't* all, and a fresh sob ripped out of me. I hid my face in my hands.

"Oh, sweetheart. I'm so sorry." Mrs. Von stepped towards me and put her arms out, then hesitated. She awkwardly patted my shoulders, like she forgot how hugs worked. "Here, come sit down."

She steered me into the kitchen and pointed me towards a barstool. I sat down and put my chin on my arms while she made a fresh pot of coffee. It seemed like an odd time of day for coffee, but I wasn't complaining. I gripped the mug and savored the heat, hoping some of the warmth would seep from my fingertips into my soul.

"Do you want any creamer?" she asked.

"No," I said, indulging in a small chuckle. "This is perfect."

She studied me. "Do you want to take your dinner in your room tonight?"

I looked up at her. "I'd really appreciate that." As much as I loved Mr. Von, I didn't have the guts to watch sterilized sitcoms with him tonight.

Her lips stretched in a sympathetic smile. "Have you told your dad about your friend? Wait." She hesitated, but before I could correct her, she barreled on. "You don't have parents, do you? But you have someone. You told me. He's..." Her face pinched as she struggled to fire neurons that weren't there.

I helped her out. "Nic. My guardian." *Your son,* I thought but didn't add.

"Yes, him." She smiled, but I could tell by the tone of her voice that she was just taking my word for it. "Have you talked to him about what's going on?"

"No," I groaned. "But I should."

I'd have to tell him. I hadn't called him yesterday, and he never let me go more than forty-eight hours without video chatting him. With a pang of guilt, I realized that I'd been trying to space out our calls more than usual over the past week. It wasn't that I didn't want to talk to him; it was just that our conversations had gotten painfully repetitive. I knew exactly what he would say every time, and some days, I just wasn't in the mood to hear it.

But he needed to know what was happening with Dad. And, in a cruel irony, he was the one person who would most understand what I was going through.

Mrs. Von nodded encouragingly. "Go on then. Oh—you have mail."

"What?" My exclamation was too loud for the room, but the situation warranted it. There was no reason I should be getting mail. First of all, paper correspondence had gone out of fashion almost fifty years ago. But more importantly, there were only a few people who knew my address, and the majority of them lived on Mars.

She slid an envelope across the counter towards me. I picked it up and almost dropped it in horror when my fingers brushed the embossed United seal. Mail from the government was the worst kind of correspondence.

It was addressed to *Ms. Andromeda Nolan*, and the return label was for one of the capitol buildings in Beijing. I swallowed a flash of panic as I flipped the envelope over.

Someone had hand-written a note on the back in calligraphic cursive.

YOU'RE STILL INVITED –ASIA

I shuddered. Asia, as she called herself, was someone with money and political influence, and that was all I knew about her. My old enemy Carnegie had been planning to sell my father—and the formula for Red Rain—to her, but she claimed she didn't need it anymore. Said it was an "unnecessary mess."

I didn't fully believe that story, but so far, she'd held true to her word. She'd gladly given me the password to unlock Dad's cryogenics tube so we could thaw him, and she'd even paid for part of the procedure. More importantly, even though she knew exactly who I was and could have me executed at any moment, she'd been nothing but respectful. She never called, never invaded my privacy, and never showed up unannounced.

And yet, she wouldn't *leave*. She texted every few days, asking how Dad was progressing. Twice she sent more money, even though I didn't need it. She even had her lawyer deliver the paperwork for some trust funds and stocks she discovered were in Andromeda's name.

She was, by all accounts, acting like my friend, and that was the last thing a United official from Beijing should be.

I gingerly sliced the seal on the envelope with my finger and pulled out a card. It was a beautiful piece of heavyweight linen, embossed with gold and inked in red. I scanned the elegant typeface:

HIS EXCELLENCE GENERAL SECRETARY MONG
REQUESTS THE HONOR OF YOUR PRESENCE
AT THE 43RD ANNUAL STATE DINNER
JULY 25TH, 2076
SUMMER PALACE, BEIJING

I ran my finger over the letters. Apparently, Asia still wanted me to come to my birthday party.

July 25th was my birthday—or, more accurately, it was Andromeda's birthday. When we met, Asia had said the state dinner was supposed to be my coming out party, my debut into high society. That was back when Mrs. Nolan and her husband Thames were planning on taking me home and making me one of them.

According to Asia, that's still where I belonged.

I shoved the invitation back in the envelope and slid it into the little black backpack that I always carried with me. "It's an invite for a sorority at school," I said in response to Mrs. Von's quizzical stare.

"Must be a fancy one if they're willing to waste paper," she remarked, and she had no idea how right she was.

I accepted the plate of food she handed to me and stood up. Thanking her, I trudged up the stairs to Cea's old bedroom. I threw my backpack on the bed and set the plate on the nightstand, then took my tablet off the charger.

As always, the screen brightened to a flurry of notifications. I wasn't allowed to have my tablet on base. It was registered to Andromeda Nolan, and even though Jayde cloaked the internet traffic, we couldn't risk having Andromeda check in anywhere near the base.

I'd gotten surprisingly used to not having a device on me all day, but Nic was less accepting. Even though he was fully aware I wouldn't be home until evening, he sent me salty texts throughout the day. In part to remind me that he disapproved of my off-the-grid lifestyle, and in part, I suspected, to make sure he was the first person I talked to when I came online.

I sat down on the bed and opened our encrypted messaging app.

YOU ONLINE?

I watched his avatar flicker green.

AM NOW

I braced myself and started a video call.

He appeared, sitting at the desk in his office. The pale Martian sky shone out the window behind him. He had one leg crossed over the other and a coffee cup in his hand, his smart blond mustache posed perfectly on the rim. He looked like the mad scientist from a bad movie, with his starched lab coat and gelled hair, and I half-expected him to start the conversation with *"I've been expecting your call."*

With a twinge in my heart, I realized our relationship would be a whole lot less complicated if he'd stayed a villain.

The stereotyped image shattered when he frowned and lowered his mug. "What happened?"

I tried to smile but failed to land the delivery. "Is it that obvious?"

"Judging by the state of your makeup, you've been crying."

I pressed a finger to my cheek and came away with a smear of mascara and eyeliner. I rubbed it and avoided looking at the camera. "We brought Dad online today."

I heard a clink and roll as he set his mug on the desk and dragged his chair closer to the monitor. "And?"

"And this is the part where you say you understand exactly how I feel." I sniffed, but the sound snagged on my throat. I tipped my head back and stared at the ceiling, hoping gravity would keep the tears in.

He was silent. I didn't explain anymore. I didn't need to.

"I'm sorry, Philadelphia," he said finally.

I knew his use of my real name was code for all the emotions for which there were no words. I accepted the offer of sympathy with a nod.

"What's the damages?" He clacked on his keyboard.

I grabbed the plate off the nightstand and poked the mound of casserole with my finger, trying to rally the courage to eat it. "Andes thinks he has about a first-grade level language skills and object recognition."

"And his memory?"

Nic may as well have put a period on the end of that sentence for all the inflection he used. He knew the answer.

I gave up and set the plate back down. "He's gone."

Nic stopped typing, and the silence brought a fresh wave of helplessness crashing down on me. This was a problem even Nic couldn't solve.

I pulled my knees to my chin, as if that could keep my reality from shattering. "Andes thinks his memories could still be in there," I offered for no reason at all.

"That's what I'm worried about."

"What?" I looked back down at the tablet.

He rubbed his goatee, parsing his words. "Remember how I said Carnegie only needed your father's brain?"

"Yeah?" I said slowly, and by the time I'd finished the word, the horrid memories came rushing back.

All he needed was the formula for Red Rain—which is in your father's memory banks somewhere...

Nic nodded. "If any of your father's memories are intact, it means Red Rain is in there, too. Just because he can't access them doesn't mean a synaptic device couldn't read them."

Any old synaptic device could read them. Your father wouldn't have to be "viable" for that to work.

I sank back against the headboard, the weight of failure squeezing the breath from my lungs. I'd sacrificed the last six months of my life trying to keep Red Rain out of the hands of the government. That was the whole reason my dad even got frozen; I'd nearly killed him trying to destroy the weapon.

Now, Red Rain was the only thing my father was good for.

"He's essentially a walking flash drive," Nic admitted. "And unfortunately, he's an even greater liability because he doesn't know who he is. If someone wearing scrubs told him he needed to submit to a brain scan, he'd probably comply."

I didn't argue. There was nothing to argue with.

"You need to come home."

The statement pierced through the haze in my mind. "Huh?"

"You need to come back to Mars."

I heard the shift in his voice, the compassion freezing over, and knew where the conversation was going. I picked the tablet up. "Nic, I can't."

"First of all, that's a grammatically incorrect use of that word. You certainly *can*; you've just chosen not to. Second of all, I don't think you have a choice anymore." He folded his arms across his chest and continued lecturing before I could get a word in edgewise. "Your father needs therapy, and lots of it. He needs to be in a secure, controlled environment. And controlled environments are one thing I specialize in."

"He could stay—" I squeaked.

"Where? On base? Surrounded by unfamiliar faces, dangerous machinery, and a questionable amount of weapons? Yes, I'm sure there's nothing that could trigger him there."

I bit my lip.

"And he absolutely can't stay at my parents," Nic continued, checking off an invisible list in the air with his fingers. "The last thing you need is *three* brainwashed adults in one house."

I sighed, purposefully loud enough for him to hear. He was right, as always. Dad needed to be in a safe environment while he recovered, and Nic's science station was the safest place I knew. My dad should be on Mars.

But that didn't mean I should be.

Nic gave me two beats to comply. "Are you booking transit tickets? Because I don't see your hands moving."

"Nic, I can't…" I grunted and tried again. "I *won't* leave. Not yet. The operation launches in three months…"

Nic swore and lurched out of his chair, leaving it to spin listlessly in frame. "How many times are we going to have this conversation?"

I felt the heat rising behind my ears. "I don't know—until you realize this is serious."

He stopped with his back to the camera. "I know *you* think this is serious, and that's what concerns me."

I opened my mouth to object, but the air died on my tongue. I knew it would be pointless, just like it had been pointless the last dozen times I'd tried to explain. No matter what I told him, no matter how hard I tried to convince him that Operation Blue Fire was necessary, he didn't care.

He didn't think I could lead the rebellion. And worse, he didn't think I should.

I looked away from the camera. This—this was why I had been avoiding our calls. "I don't want to have this conversation tonight."

"Good," he chirped without turning around, "because there's nothing to discuss. You're coming home, Andromeda."

I pinched my eyes shut. "Nic, please, not right now—"

"No," he snapped, a metric ton of anger crammed into the word. He whipped back around to face me. "I'm done. I feel like I've been very patient…"

That's not exactly how I'd describe you.

"…and let you play out your fantasy for the past month, but it's over." He gripped the back of his desk chair until his knuckles went white. "You are not a hero, Andromeda."

His words struck like a whip across my back. "I'm not—I'm not trying to be," I squeaked. *Is that what you think of me?*

"Oh really?" he sneered, tone like vinegar on a wound. "Then why are you still there? Why did you even go back to Earth?"

Please stop, I wanted to beg, but couldn't. I knew the answer. I knew my sins, but he listed them anyway.

"You went back because you thought you could fix everything. You thought you could save your dad. And look what happened."

Tears shot to my eyes. I dropped the tablet on the bed and wrapped my arms around my chest.

He was right. This was all my fault.

"They don't need you, Andromeda. They can do this without you." He made a herculean effort to soften his voice, but it just made him sound fake. "Your focus needs to be on your family right now."

I closed my eyes. *Please, just stop talking. You've made your point.*

He let out his breath. "You'll buy transit tickets tonight. I want to see the receipts."

I slapped my palms down on the blanket. "What, you don't trust me anymore?"

He showed no mercy. "The appropriate response was 'yessir.'"

I flinched. "Yessir," I whispered, and then ended the call before he could see me cry.

4

"Captain on the bridge."

The command room on the top floor of the base was full when I arrived the next morning. Everyone who needed to know—Ephesus, Tower, Jayde, Lev, Mrs. Nolan—was there, along with a plethora of soldiers. I rubbed my arm nervously as they all saluted. At least I wouldn't have to repeat myself.

"We're ready for you to stream," Jayde said, walking around to the other side of the glittering control module that dominated the center of the room. "I want you to talk about—"

"No," I said, and flinched when he jerked back. I swallowed and forced the rest out before I could stop myself. "I'm not streaming today. There's been a change of plans."

"What?" he barked.

Ephesus walked over, his brow furrowed in concern. "What's wrong, Phil?"

I took a deep breath and looked up at him. "We're going back to Mars."

There were gasps and muttered exclamations—some foul—from around the room. Tower shifted but said nothing. Jayde wasted no time in losing his temper. "You can't leave! We launch in three months, and I—"

"We can still do this!" I shouted to match his volume, mostly to convince myself. "I can record videos from Mars."

Even Nic had said as much. He'd texted me a few hours after we'd hung up, as if it had finally dawned on him that he was being a heartless jerk.

IF YOU REALLY FEEL THE NEED TO DO THIS, YOU CAN STREAM VIDEOS FROM HERE. THE STUDIO IS STILL SET UP

He was right, but it was too late for damage control. I didn't reply to the message.

The bickering continued around the room. "Why are you leaving?" my uncle asked. His tone was flat, as was the expression on his face.

"Dad needs a stable environment while he goes through therapy," I explained, reciting exactly what Nic had said, "and Mars is the safest place for him."

Ephesus slid his arm protectively over my shoulder. I searched his face for approval; he looked relieved, if anything. "She's right. Dad can't stay here, and we need to be there for him while he gets treatment. Phil can record videos remotely." He scanned the room, as if daring anyone to argue with his judgment as big brother. "After all, she started on Mars—she can finish there. No one will know the difference."

"We'll know," Lev whispered from where he stood in the shadows. He squinted and blinked, as if he couldn't decide whether to be angry or betrayed. I turned away, unable to look him in the eye.

"I'm trying to win a war here." Jayde slapped his hand on the control panel, eliciting a screech from the computer. "I can't have my revolutionary leader *on another planet*."

"Then get a new leader," Stanyard spat.

Jayde ignored him, his fierce eyes still on me. "And why do you have to go? Your father doesn't need you anymore."

Ephesus stiffened. I was too heartbroken to object.

"As the only one in this room with any medical knowledge, I strongly disagree," Mrs. Nolan spoke for the first time. She crossed her arms and glared at Jayde. "She's been through enough. Let her go home and take care of her family."

"And what about the rest of us, huh?" Jayde threw his arms out and turned around, including the entire room in his statement. "What about the rest of us who suffer every day because the United decided we're not part of the system? What about all those people who agreed to join the operation? Are you going to hide out on Mars while the rest of us risk our lives?"

He swiveled back to face me. I returned his stare, unable to answer him. That was exactly what I'd be doing.

He snorted. He reached back and punched a button on the dashboard, and the playback from the camera appeared on the giant monitor that hung from the ceiling. There I was, larger than life, the circles under my eyes forming dark shadows in the dank lighting of the command room. The "go live" button flickered in the corner of the screen.

Jayde held his finger over the key. "You want to tell your followers that? You want to tell everyone that Blue Fire is abandoning them?"

Tower grabbed his wrist. "Don't be stupid. Let's think this through."

Jayde pulled his hand back. "Oh, I think she's thought about it plenty. She's already made up her mind, can't you tell?"

The room was silent. Ephesus squeezed my shoulder.

Jayde spat in my direction. "You're a coward."

"Shut up!" Stanyard yelled, and hit him in the back of the head.

Jayde barely flinched. He just reached up and ruffled his hair back into place.

Stanyard muttered something else under his breath, then walked over and touched my shoulder. "Let's go, Phil."

"Don't listen to him," Ephesus agreed, taking my other arm and following us.

I allowed them to lead me from the room, my eyes on the floor. I couldn't tell them that I thought Jayde was right.

*

"You're sure you'll be okay while I'm gone?"

"It's only for a week," I reminded him, and tried to keep the fatigue out of my voice. Ephesus hadn't had many opportunities to play the protective older brother over the past few years, and he was trying to make up for lost time with this conversation.

We were standing on the sidewalk outside the transit hub having a repeat of the same argument we'd had on the ride over, and the night before, and the day before that. Per Nic's advice, we'd booked separate transit flights in case one of us aroused suspicion. So far, Ephesus hadn't had any trouble buying a ticket or registering a new phone under his temporary file, but all of us were wanted for crimes worthy of death. We couldn't be too careful.

Mrs. Nolan wanted to keep Dad under for a little while longer, and then he would need at least a couple days of physical therapy before he would be well enough to fly. He and I would be leaving in about a week.

Nic was none too happy about the delay, but he couldn't argue with doctor's orders.

Ephesus scrunched his nose, like the whole situation smelled foul. "I don't like leaving before you."

He'd made that abundantly clear, but he'd forgotten that I was just as stubborn as he was. "I'm not leaving Dad."

"And why do you get to pick? I'm eight years older than you!" He flapped his hands, as if the wild motion could make me change my mind.

I crossed my arms. "Because I'm paying."

Stanyard, who waited a comfortable distance away next to his car, snickered.

Ephesus blanched. "You've been spending too much time with Nic."

I rolled my eyes. *You have no idea.*

Ephesus finally acquiesced with a grunt. "I'll be offline until I land. So if anything happens, call Nic."

"Of course," I fudged. Nic was the last person I wanted to call. I didn't plan to talk to him until I got back to Mars, and maybe not even then.

Ephesus looked over my head and pointed at Stanyard. "I'm trusting you."

Stanyard saluted.

I pushed Ephesus's arm down. "Tell Cea I said hi."

He grinned. "Oh, I will." The sparkle returned to his eyes, suggesting he would also tell her a lot more. I copied his smile. There were a few good things about moving back to Mars.

Ephesus wrapped me in a hug. "Stay safe, stick with Stanyard, and I'll see you soon."

"Yes, yes, and yes." I savored his hug for a moment more, then pushed him away. "Now go. You'll miss your flight."

He grabbed his suitcase off the sidewalk and waved at Stanyard, then turned and jogged towards the revolving doors. I waited until he had blended with the crowd and disappeared out of sight before I turned back to Stanyard.

He opened the passenger door for me. "Want to go back to base?"

"No," I admitted as I slid in. Base was the last place I wanted to be right now. I didn't want to see Jayde or record another video where I lied through my teeth about how we were all in this together. "But Jayde is expecting me."

Stanyard shut the door and got behind the wheel. After glancing to make sure there was no one waiting behind us, he leaned over and touched my knee. "If it helps, I think you're making the right decision."

"Thanks," I said, even though I meant the exact opposite. Three of the people I trusted most in the world thought going back to Mars was the right thing to do.

Then why did it feel so wrong?

Stanyard said nothing more and took his hand away to start the car. A few raindrops plunked off the hood as we pulled away from the awning and merged into traffic. I leaned my arm on the door and watched out the window as the rain increased to a downpour. The city blurred into an abstract painting as the lights reflected off the puddles on the sidewalk. I closed my eyes and let the pounding on the roof lull me into prayer.

What do you want me to do, God?

Nic wanted me to go back to Mars—that was my answer, right? After all, according to him, I never should have left. But the more I tried to accept that logic, the more I felt haunted by the fear that I was throwing something precious away.

I replayed the last six months in my mind, tripping over all the coincidence and happenstance that could only be called a miracle. Red Rain, Carnegie, the Nolans, Dad, the truth about my mother's death. All the horrible and tragic things that had somehow collided into this, into me becoming Blue Fire. God had taken my father's failure and turned it into a revolution—that had to be God, right?

I reached into my backpack and pulled out the star of David pin Lev had given me. I twisted it in my fingers, rubbing the tarnished metal, and remembered his words.

For such a time as this.

I jerked out of my stupor when we drove into a tunnel, cutting off the sound of rain. I looked up and watched the yellow fluorescents whip past.

And then, suddenly, there was a flash of blue paint on the concrete wall.

I twisted around and caught a glimpse just before the graffiti passed out of sight around the corner.

It was a thunderbird.

The image was unmistakable: The crude form of a hawk-like bird, its wings spread wide in defiance. In its claws was clutched a jagged bolt of lightning.

Stanyard craned his neck to look in the rearview mirror. "I'm surprised they haven't painted over that yet. Must be fresh."

I didn't respond. I closed my fist around the pin.

It was still pouring when we got back to base. I checked on Dad, then reluctantly went up to the command room. It was mercifully empty except for a couple of nameless guards.

I went to the control module in the center of the room and pulled up the streaming app. But instead of launching a video, I navigated to the search bar and typed in my name.

The government worked tirelessly to block any content featuring my name or callsign, but automatic filters weren't perfect and the internet was creative. It wasn't hard to find a repost of my latest stream that had escaped the censors.

The views were over five million, and that was just on this one repost. I scrolled through the lengthy comments section. Some people mocked me, but most were supportive. There was a user who claimed to be thirteen who said I was an inspiration. There was another teen who claimed he and his friends were going to walk out of class on operation day. Several users were throwing coded messages back and forth, coordinating a demonstration of some sort. There were comments in Hebrew, Arabic, Mandarin. And all of them were punctuated with emojis of lightning bolts and fire.

"They trust you."

I jumped and turned. Jayde stood in the shadows behind me, his face faintly lit by the blue glow from the monitors.

I looked back at the screen. "I know."

"I trust you."

I glanced up as he came to stand beside me. "Really?" I'd never gotten that impression from Jayde. He appreciated my ability to rally the crowds, but we weren't friends. We didn't need to be.

He nodded. "I'm sorry I yelled at you the other day. I know that if you say you'll record videos from Mars, you will."

"I promise," I assured him.

"But," he said, and I flinched. There was always a "but" with Jayde.

He sighed and randomly flicked a slider in the soundboard. "I know you can do so much more than record videos."

I frowned. "Like what?"

He opened his mouth to respond, but we were interrupted by one of the guards. "Sir," he said, stepping between us, "I'm sorry, but there's someone at reception asking to see Blue Fire."

I straightened. "Me?"

Jayde's hand instinctively touched his holster. "Who is it?"

The guard hesitated, then handed a tablet to Jayde.

He took one look at the screen and swore. "What is she doing here?"

"She?" I repeated.

He didn't answer. He shoved the tablet back at the guard and took off at a jog. I raced to keep up.

We took the elevator to the first floor. The base operated out of the shell of a defunct business, and as far as the public knew, this office building was still staffed with a bunch of while-collar salesmen and accountants. To keep up that façade, reception had been converted into an elaborate security checkpoint. From the outside, it looked benign enough, with the potted plants and bored secretary, while armed guards watched everything from behind one-way mirrors.

A girl about my age was leaning over the counter, arguing with the receptionist, but I couldn't see her face from beneath her dripping hood. Jayde shoved past the guard at the door and burst out into the lobby without ceremony.

"What are you doing here?" he demanded.

I came out behind him. The girl straightened. "I didn't come to see you," she spat at Jayde.

I choked on my next breath when I recognized her voice. *It can't be.*

I walked around the counter. The girl turned towards me and flicked her hood back, revealing her face.

Mira.

5

After three beats of awkward staring, I realized Jayde was asking the right questions.

"What are you doing here?" I exclaimed, and hoped she would give me a long, detailed answer to that question. Last I'd heard, Mira Dass had run away from home, abandoning her brother and dropping off the grid. Stanyard hadn't seen any activity on her file in months, and he'd been watching it religiously.

She didn't take the hint. "I'm here to see you."

And not your own brother? I thought, swallowing rage. Stanyard had been heartbroken when Mira left. He'd spent weeks trying to find her, and he still blamed himself for her loss. He wouldn't admit that in so many words, but I could see it in his eyes, the way he avoided saying her name.

The revelation that she'd been alive and well this whole time was filling me with the unladylike urge to hit her. I chose to use my words instead.

"I'm flattered," I snapped, "but there's several problems with that statement, first and foremost being that my name is not Stanyard."

She leaned back against the counter and arched an eyebrow. "You've changed."

"So have you." I studied her and tried to decide if that was a good thing. She'd chopped her hair; half of it was shaved, and the other half fell across her face in a sharp pixie cut. It was dyed an unnatural shade of black with a pink stripe. She had a stud in her nose and at least five in her ears, and a giant dragon tattoo covered the right side of her body. It looked like the animal was swallowing her arm and sinking its teeth into her neck.

And as she stared at me, I could see that there was nothing behind her eyes. Not even anger.

"What happened, Mira?" I whispered.

"Nothing." She shrugged. "I got out of camp and found a new life—just like you."

"But…" I retraced everything Stanyard had told me, trying to find out where things had gone wrong. "Stanyard said you ran off and married a soldier…"

The words died on my tongue. I stared at her dragon tattoo, then looked up at Jayde.

The Green Dragon.

"You guys are *married?*" I screeched.

Jayde snorted.

"We were going to be," Mira snapped, fixing Jayde with a glare that could boil water. She rubbed her bare ring finger in a gesture that was not lost on anyone in the room.

I grimaced. "And why didn't you tell Stanyard? You knew he was looking for her!" I directed the accusation at Jayde, even though I wasn't sure who to blame more.

Jayde shrugged callously. "She wasn't even talking to *me* then—we'd already broken up."

I turned my frown on Mira.

She avoided my eyes. "I didn't want him to know—and I still don't." She stood up and pushed herself away from the counter. "I'm not staying."

"And neither am I. I'm going to go find him." I spun for the door, trying to decide whether to cry or be sick.

"No, Phil, wait!" She lunged forward and caught my arm. "Please, just listen. It's important."

I tried to wrench my arm from her grasp and realized with a flash of shame that I couldn't. *This is why you need to train more.* I settled for glaring at her. "What's important is telling Stanyard the truth."

She met my eyes. "It's about our old camp."

I stopped.

She mercifully let go of me to reach inside her jacket. "The district office just issued an emergency order to have the entire camp relocated—tomorrow. Everyone's getting shipped out in the morning."

Jayde's cold warning flashed through my mind.

Things are changing. The government is tired of paying for the room and board of a bunch of noncompliants. There's talk of relocation, of condensing the camps—or worse.

"To where?" Jayde grunted the question I was afraid to ask.

Mira pulled a scuffed flash drive out of her pocket and twisted it in her fingers. "China."

I muttered in tongues, too horrified to speak in English. No one else said anything. We all knew a flight to China, the center of the United government, was a one-way trip.

And Stanyard and Mira's parents still lived in that camp.

"I'm not exactly sure where in China they're taking them, but it's definitely a labor camp." She held the flash drive out to Jayde. "I have a copy of the order and several text messages verifying the pickup time."

Jayde opened his mouth, but Mira put up both hands to stop him. "Don't ask me where I got them, because it was *extremely* illegal. But I can promise you, my source knows what they're talking about." She stuffed her hands in her pockets and flicked her eyes around the room, as if she were afraid her informant was going to leap out from behind a potted plant.

"But why?" I cried. "I mean, why now? And why our camp? There's less than a hundred people in there."

She turned to me, her face tightened in a glare. "Because of you."

I took a step back.

"You might not know this," she continued, the concession spoken without any mercy, "but they've been rounding up everyone who ever knew you and interrogating them."

I gripped the edge of the reception desk. "What for?"

"Why do you think?" she sighed, as if my ignorance was exhausting. "To try and figure out where you are—and if that doesn't work, find out what makes you tick."

The room toppled, and a wave of anguish tried to force my stomach up my throat. I bent over the desk, searching for my balance, but I couldn't find it. The United was interrogating—torturing—people because of me. This was my fault.

Nic was right. I wasn't a hero.

"They had Dad and Mom in yesterday." Mira's words were slow and purposeful, driving the guilt in like a nail. "Kept them in that room for twelve hours straight."

"I'm—I'm sorry," I gasped, more to God than to her.

She shrugged. "I got off easy. I left before you did, so they correctly assumed I didn't know anything."

Jayde stepped forward, shattering the tension between us. "Why didn't you tell me sooner?" he asked Mira. His face was softened in an expression that made me believe they had in fact had a relationship once. "I probably could have gotten in on the session with your parents. I was able to bail Aid out of his."

Mira didn't have an answer to that, but I had several follow-up questions. "Wait." I stood up, my gravity recentering as a weight dropped to my stomach. "You knew? You knew they were interrogating people?"

He blinked, unashamed. "What would you have done if I told you? Stopped recording? Canceled the operation?"

I snapped my mouth shut with a click. *I definitely wouldn't have let them keep torturing my friends.*

"Exactly." He folded his arms. "These things happen in war, and I couldn't have you distracted—"

"No," I snapped. When he looked like he was about to mouth off again, I repeated myself. "No. Not in my war. We're going to save them."

He frowned, but Mira beat him to words. "What?"

"We're going to break them out," I said, and only after the statement left my mouth did I realize what I was proposing. I forged ahead before I could attach any emotions or fear to my thoughts. "We can't let them get shipped off to China. We have to intercept them. How are they transporting them? How many guards?"

The questions were directed at Mira, and it took her several breaths before she complied. "It's not terrible—a couple of prison vans, maybe a dozen guards."

"We can handle that," I declared, and turned to Jayde for confirmation. "Remember when you broke me out of Thames's headquarters? You redirected the van."

He shook his head, but it was a rapid, recalibrating shake, not a doubtful one. "It's too late to forge orders—this has clearly already gone through the chain of command. We're better off breaking them out tonight, before they load them up."

"Okay then," I replied, and that was that.

Jayde arched an eyebrow. "So?"

I threw my arms out. "So what? Let's go." If I put any more logical thought into this, I might reconsider, and we didn't have time for that.

"Are those your orders, Blue Fire?" he returned with a bow of his head.

I sighed and realized it was on me to pull the trigger. This was my choice. This was my fight.

"Yes," I repeated, straightening and planting my feet apart. "We're breaking them out tonight. That's an order."

His face split in a grin. "Yessir."

6

"I'm not going with you."

"Yes, you are," I argued, and yelped when I stabbed myself in the eye with my mascara. If I thought dressing up as Philadelphia would mean less makeup, I was wrong.

After I had debriefed the other commanders on the plan, I'd gone home for dinner so I wouldn't upset the Vons' routine. The last thing I needed was the police out looking for me because Mrs. Von lost her marbles. So I'd eaten dinner like a normal person, packed a bag with a change of clothes and makeup, and told them I was going to sleep over at a friend's house. Mira even picked me up and corroborated my story.

Now she and I were locked in a bathroom on base, where we'd spent the last hour and a half putting Philadelphia back together. I'd sprayed my hair with temporary brown dye and pinned it up under a scarf so you couldn't tell how long it was. I'd plastered over the piercings in my ears and concealed the scratches and bruises I'd earned while training. In their place, I'd given myself a new identity marker: a fake thunderbird tattoo, drawn on the upper part of my arm with a fine-tipped pen.

"No, I'm going home." Mira twirled my powder brush in her fingers, her eyes avoiding mine in the mirror. "You don't need my help."

"No, but your parents do." I tossed my mascara in my bag and turned to face her. "Mira, please. What's wrong?"

"Nothing," she said for at least the sixth time that evening.

"Stanyard would beg to differ," I muttered.

After no small amount of badgering from both Jayde and me, Mira had agreed to come up to the command deck and tell us what she knew about the relocation order. Stanyard burst into the room moments later. He did exactly what I expected him to do: scream Mira's name at the top of his lungs and grab her in a hug.

She did the exact opposite of what I expected her to do. She didn't even hug him back. She just gave him a weird pat on the shoulder and then pushed him away, cutting off any more inquisition with a cold, "It's fine, I'm safe."

I almost regretted forcing the reunion when I saw the soul shatter behind Stanyard's eyes. He'd always suspected that Mira didn't want to see him again, but I think, up until that moment, he'd held onto a sliver of hope, the private belief that there was some other explanation. That there was something, anything, outside of her control keeping her away.

In the cold silence of the command room, as she turned her back on him and faced the monitor, we all realized the truth. Mira had stayed away because she wanted to.

"I just don't want to talk to him right now." She flicked the brush bristles.

"Then talk to me." I opened my arms and softened my voice. "You always used to be able to talk to me."

I'm not sure why I thought that would work. All she did was glance at me out of the corner of her eye and snort. "I'm just... not ready."

"Ready for what? To be a family again?" I scoffed, and too late realized how harsh that sounded.

She tipped her head back, her cropped hair sliding across her ear. "We were never a family."

Grief crusted with rage rolled through me. "That's a lie, and you know it. I know your father wasn't the greatest…"

"You have *no* idea," she hissed.

I ignored the comment. "…but one thing I know: Stanyard always cared about you. Everything he did was for you."

She looked down at the floor, and I thought I'd found the crack in her armor. "That's why you left camp, isn't it? You're the one that wanted to go."

She straightened and pushed herself off the counter. "Yes, I was. And do you want to know why?"

My conscience writhed. I could tell by the tone of her voice that I'd ruined the conversation, but she didn't wait for an answer. "I left because I was tired of dealing with stupid, self-righteous people like my dad. Like you."

I sucked in my breath.

She glared back at me, eyes like knives. "You always thought you could fix everyone. Thought that if you played the peacemaker, were just so sweet and kind and forgiving to everyone, that you could make it all better." Her voice dripped with syrup. "Well, you can't. You can't fix the government, you can't fix Stanyard, and you can't fix me. So stop trying. I *don't* want your help."

Jayde knocked on the door and asked if we were ready, but I couldn't answer him. I couldn't move. All I could hear were Nic's words echoing in my head, around and around and around.

You are not a hero, Andromeda.

"We'll be right out," Mira called. She grabbed a pair of gloves and pulled them on, hiding the dragon tail that was drawn on her wrist. "I'm going to help you, because despite what you might think, I don't want my parents to die. But after that, I'm leaving. And if you have any decency, you'll let me walk away."

I did just that. She threw the door open and walked into the hall, and I just stood there, staring at the door until long after it had shut.

The team met us in the parking garage. Stanyard stared at his sister, gaping like a fish as he tried and failed several times to say something.

I gave him a less-than-subtle shake of my head. He finally shut his mouth and clenched his jaw.

"Put these in." Jayde dropped a pair of earbuds into my hand, then walked around the circle and distributed pairs to the other soldiers. "I want codenames only. Except for Ms. Smyrna over here, the government doesn't know our real names, and I'd like to keep it that way."

"Uh, what if we don't remember our code names?" a familiar voice chirped.

"Do we get to pick new ones? Say yes! I wanna pick a new name!" his partner screeched at a volume much too loud for the acoustics of the parking garage.

"John? Dowe?" I scanned the lot and spotted them a few cars away, dangling out the back of a suspicious white van. It looked like the kind of vehicle you'd commit a crime in, and for better or for worse, John and Dowe definitely looked like the strangers my parents warned me about. They were old enough to be grandparents, and they looked so creepily identical that I often wondered if they were the result of a failed cloning experiment.

The one who was probably John put his hand up. "No, no, I want to be Dowe this time. Except I'm going to spell it D-o-e and really throw people off."

"Basic," the real Dowe muttered. At least, process of elimination would suggest that he was the real Dowe. "You're going to make a terrible me."

"Your fault for being such a poor role model."

Jayde pinched the bridge of his nose. "Who invited these two?"

"I did." Tower stepped up, his jacket slung over his shoulder. "They volunteered. And besides, we needed the van."

"Does it even drive?" Stanyard questioned. He pointed to the massive patches of rust that were eating away at the bottom of the vehicle, like the van had been gnawed on by a shark.

"Oh, don't worry about that." John flapped his hand. "It was stuck in the ocean for six months."

"I don't think—" Jayde started to object.

"They're coming," I declared. John and Dowe were arguably insane, and I definitely wouldn't trust them with a loaded gun, but they were excellent at staging breakouts and distractions. And that's exactly what we needed.

"Fine, but you're riding with me," Jayde snapped, and I didn't argue.

"Your loss," John muttered. "This will definitely be the fun-vee."

Jayde clapped his hands, the sharp sound summoning all the attention in the room, and raised his voice. "All right people, listen up. This should be a very simple extraction. We've got about seventy individuals, most of whom are adults and should get with the program pretty quick once they realize what's going on."

He turned and gestured at the row of mismatched vans and SUVs filling the lot. "We're going to divide and conquer. Each vehicle is going to take ten refugees. Drivers, as soon as you're full, head out. Don't wait. You're all going in different directions and taking them to different drop-off points. If we arouse suspicion, I want the other teams to bail. I'm not losing the whole batch because one of us gets pulled over for a random traffic stop."

That's not going to happen, I prayed. *We're all going to make it.*

"Our latest intel suggests that this place is low security." Tower walked into the middle of the circle, keying on a tablet. He set it on the floor, and it projected a map on the ceiling of the parking garage where everyone could see it. I stared at the network of narrow roads and tiny homes and fought down a sickening sense of familiarity.

"Our biggest concerns are the watchtower and the fact that the only entrance is the front gate." Tower pointed to the north edge of the map. "However, that information was collected before Phil made herself famous. We know for a fact the United has been questioning her neighbors; they could have also upped security in case she came home."

I felt the shift in the room, the change in gravity as everyone looked at me. I glanced down and rubbed my arm, trying to hide the goosebumps.

"So be prepared for surprises," Lev grunted from beside me.

Jayde nodded. "Right. Now I've got a friend at the electric company who can cut the power for us—but there's two problems with that. One, we can only leave it off for about twenty minutes. Any longer and the government is likely to dispatch police as backup in case someone tries something. Two, when the power goes out at the camp, the backup generator will kick in and autolock the gate."

A murmur rippled around the group. I wrapped my arms around my chest and prayed harder.

"The plan is to use those twenty minutes of darkness to scale the wall and get everyone ready to move." Jayde circled the projection, tracing the perimeter with his finger. "Tower's team is going to break into the watchtower and take out the guards while the rest of us herd the evacuees towards the front gate. When the power comes online, Tower will use his knowledge of the system to radio an okay so the government doesn't send reinforcements. Then we'll open the gate and load everyone out."

"But the security cameras will be online," Stanyard objected.

"I'll be the only one watching," Tower assured him, "but corporate will review the footage after they realize what happened. So hoods up, heads down, and absolutely no electronics."

Jayde held up his phone for emphasis. "This is a blackout operation. No devices except our radios. I don't want anyone leaving a mark."

"Except me." I stepped forward, welcoming the shift in attention this time. I shrugged off my jacket, stripping down to a black tank top and revealing my hand-drawn tattoo. "I want them to know I was there."

Someone gasped. Stanyard gripped my elbow. "But Phil—"

I turned to him. "I know they're doing this because of me. The interrogations, the relocation—it's all to get back at me."

His kind eyes searched me. "It's not your fault."

"Maybe not." I shifted my gaze to Mira. "But I'm going to show them that it won't work."

She arched an eyebrow.

Stanyard turned pleading eyes to Tower, as if expecting him to stop me. But my uncle just folded his arms across his chest and smiled.

"All right, let's move out!" Jayde shouted.

"Anyone else want to ride in the fun-vee?" John hollered. "We have snacks!"

"They might be stale, though…"

"It's fruit leather. It was made for the apocalypse."

Jayde approached me, snapping the clip into a small pistol. "Here, you need this." He grabbed my wrist and forced the gun into my hand before I could refuse.

I held it away from my body, resisting the urge to drop it. "Jayde, you know I can't shoot."

"You can, you just won't," he barked, and sounded an awful lot like Nic.

He wasn't wrong, though. I did know *how* to shoot. Jayde had been making me practice in the range almost daily, and muscle memory was starting to override my hesitancy. I'd learned to handle the recoil, and my aim wasn't terrible.

But no amount of practice could silence the horror that screamed through my system every time the weapon fired. Each time the explosion pierced the protective headphones, all I could think about was Thames, and Carnegie, and Ambrose—all the people who had threatened me with guns or died by them.

I couldn't be like them. I couldn't kill.

"Don't worry, I'll shoot first." Stanyard checked his own pistol, then stuffed it in the pocket of his jeans. I could see he was carrying one in each pocket, and he probably had another in his coat. "I'll be right beside you the whole time."

"And I've got your back." Lev appeared at my other arm, adjusting the strap of his rifle.

I offered him a grateful smile. Checking to make sure the safety was on, I slid the gun in my pocket and tried to ignore the weight against my thigh.

Closing my eyes, I took a deep breath, and another, filling my lungs until the air drove the anxiety away. *You can do this.* Jayde was right; it was a simple extraction. And even if it wasn't, it was the right thing to do.

I'd blown up a lab to save my family. Now it was time to save Stanyard's.

7

I never thought I'd make it home.

I sat in the backseat of Jayde's SUV, buckled safely between Stanyard and Lev, as we raced through the suburbs of Boston. At first, the sleeping neighborhoods were cold, unfamiliar, the generic houses blending into a domestic blur. But then we turned a corner, and I recognized that park, that convenience store, that apartment with the faded *Now Leasing* sign that hadn't been changed in years. I began to anticipate the turns, brace myself for the bumps in the road, as if my whole body were slipping into a trance. I probably could have driven us the rest of the way as muscle memory took me down a path I had traveled so many times before.

And I hated it.

The familiarity wasn't comforting; it was suffocating. My body didn't just remember the directions—it also remembered the fear, the pain, the abuse. Every block we passed, it felt like the air was getting thinner and the car was getting narrower, as if we were already behind the containment camp walls. I felt like I was slipping, falling—shackling myself with chains I had tried so hard to forget.

I can't go back.

I reached out and grasped Stanyard's hand, desperate to keep my head above water. He weakly squeezed my fingers, his palm clammy. I glanced at him and realized he had gone pale. Sweat trickled down the side of his face as he stared out the window, his whole body rigid.

"You okay?" I asked, even though I knew the answer. This used to be Stanyard's home, too.

"Yeah," he said, but he sounded like he couldn't catch his breath. "Just… trying to figure out what to say to my dad."

My heart broke as the pain of that day came rushing back: the day Stanyard and Mira left camp. I remembered the sickening horror as we all stood in the parking lot at school while they informed us that they'd packed their bags and left without saying goodbye. I remembered wanting to scream and call after them but not being able to find the words. I remembered feeling like I was sinking into the concrete as I watched Stanyard walk away, turning his back on his family, God, and me.

But Stanyard had changed. The Stanyard I knew came back. He'd come back to me, and he'd come back to God in powerful ways even I didn't understand. Surely, he could come back to his dad.

I wove our fingers together, anchoring my hold on his hand. "Just tell him what you told me," I said, remembering how he'd knelt on the lab floor and given me the chance to forgive or reject him.

He shook his head. "It's not the same. It was… easier with you."

"Why?" I demanded. If anything, I would have thought it would be easier to apologize to his dad. All he had to do was tell his dad that he was sorry he'd left home, and Mr. Dass would forgive him, I was sure. Me, I'd been a traumatized mess and had *hit* Stanyard when he'd tried to apologize.

Stanyard couldn't quantify his feelings. "It's... it's different with you," he mumbled, and I caught the inflection behind his voice.

I gripped his hand and felt my own pulse thrumming against my palm. "Why?" I asked again. When he avoided my eyes, I repeated myself, louder. "Why am I different, Stanyard?"

I knew the answer. But I had to hear it from him. I had to know I wasn't imagining things, reading nuance that wasn't there.

He finally looked at me, face scrunched in annoyance as if he knew exactly what I was doing. "Because I like you, Phil."

I sucked in my breath as those five words displaced a lifetime of rejection. My head spun as a thousand prayers and timid daydreams collided. There was so much I wanted to say, and suddenly I couldn't find the words for any of it.

Jayde glanced at us in the rearview mirror and arched an eyebrow.

Stanyard noticed and ended the moment. He pulled his hand from my grasp and turned back to face the window. "Besides, it's different with Dad because... well, he's kind of the reason I left. And I don't think he's figured that out yet."

I remembered Mira's bitter accusation and wondered, for the first time, if Mr. Dass had expressed his anger with more than just words.

Jayde braked at a red light. "We're almost there. Hoods up."

He yanked a ski mask over his head, not that he needed any help looking intimidating. Lev snapped on a pair of night vision googles and tied a handkerchief over his nose. Stanyard pulled the hood of his jacket up.

I couldn't see his face anymore, so I reached out with my words. "Well, if you can't forgive him, at least forgive yourself."

Jayde hovered at the intersection even after the light turned green. "Ten seconds."

Stanyard turned back to me. "For what?"

"For leaving."

At that moment, the power went out, plunging the entire block into darkness.

"It's go time," Jayde hissed, and slammed on the gas.

I braced myself against the passenger seat as we whipped around the corner, headlights off. The SUV's proximity sensor screamed in agony as Jayde barely avoided the shadowy forms of parked cars.

I felt my anxiety building like heat in an oven. I focused on taking deep breaths through my nose, forcing a prayer out with each exhale.

Holy Spirit, pave the way. The guards will be distracted and easy to take out. Everyone will be calm and cooperative. And the police will not investigate.

Jayde slowed the vehicle to a crawl. We cleared the last building, and there it was: Street 17 Containment Camp.

I craned my neck to look out the windshield. It seemed smaller than I remembered, the concrete wall somehow less imposing. The silhouette of the guard tower stood illuminated against the moon, the one-way mirrored windows reflecting the pale light like dead eyes. The panel next to the gate glowed yellow as it flashed a warning about low power.

Jayde rolled down the window and listened. The only sound was the hum of our engine and a dog barking several streets over. There were no alarms going off, no distant police sirens.

I unbuckled my seatbelt. *Thank you, Jesus.*

The other vehicles in our caravan converged from the side streets, taking up station on each corner of the building. Jayde parked next to John and Dowe's white van on the south side of the complex. Stanyard helped me out of the car.

John tipped his head back and admired the wall. "So this is your place, eh, Phil?"

"No wonder she never invited us over for dinner," Dowe muttered.

Jayde cupped his hand over his ear. "Tower, are you in?"

"Climbing the stairs now," Tower responded over the radio, sounding like he was running. "Guard at the front door neutralized."

"Be careful," a voice I didn't recognize chimed in. "There's only one other guard up here, which could mean there's one in the streets doing rounds."

"Copy," Jayde said, and nodded at me. "Stay close."

With the help of another guard, Lev dragged an apparatus from the car and dropped it near the wall. "Clear!" the other guard hissed, and cranked the lever. With a snap, a grappling hook shot from the machine and flew over the wall, dragging a ladder behind it. It dropped with a dull *thunk* on the other side of the wall.

Lev tested the hold, then scrambled up the ladder with enviable agility. I watched it buck and twist under his weight and tried not to be sick.

He crouched on the top of the wall and scanned the streets below, his googles autofocusing in the dim light. Then he waved his arm at us.

Jayde gestured to me. "After you, captain."

I swallowed. Stanyard touched my shoulder. "I'll be right behind you."

I nodded rapidly to anchor my courage and gripped the ladder before I could reconsider. I climbed as fast as I could, thinking only about grabbing each rung in order, ignoring the burn of the swaying rope on my palms.

Lev grabbed my hand and helped me onto the top of the wall. I knelt there, catching my breath, and for the briefest moment took in the view. There was my old neighborhood, an austere network of tiny concrete boxes laid out in strict rows. It looked like a graveyard without the lights on, each house representing the headstone of the family who lived inside. Had I really called this place home for nearly six years?

Lev gripped my arm as I lowered my foot onto the ladder on the other side. Thankfully climbing down was a lot easier than climbing up.

I dropped into the alley behind the first row of homes and heard Stanyard scrambling down behind me. Jayde's voice came over the radio. "We've got ten minutes, people! Get your assigned rows to the gate. Blue Fire, I want you in the middle of the road where people can see you."

"Copy," I hissed. After glancing to make sure the alley was empty, I slipped in the gap between two houses and darted for the main road.

I stepped out onto the sidewalk—and someone grabbed me from behind. I choked on a scream as a gloved closed over my mouth.

"They told me you'd come back," a gravelly voice grunted in my ear. I recognized him as Lieutenant Clint, my old warden.

Someone shrieked a warning on the radio. I fought against him as adrenaline pounded in my ears. He gripped me to him, his arms like a viper. "About time you came home, isn't it, Miss—"

The threat ended in a groan. His grip loosened, and I jerked away. I whipped around and watched him drop to the ground with a thud, unconscious.

Stanyard stood behind him, the hilt of his gun raised. "I told you I'd shoot first. You okay?"

I nodded, fighting a wave of embarrassment. *You walked right into that one. Get it together! They're counting on you!*

Stanyard stripped the lieutenant of his weapons. He tossed one to Lev and one to Jayde, who came out of the alley behind us. Jayde cocked the rifle appreciatively, then jerked his head. "Watts and John Dowe, you take this row. Augustine and Blue Fire, follow me."

He took off at a run, and Stanyard and I followed. We came around the corner to the next street, where Mira and several other guards were already banging down doors. There was commotion and crying and hushed yells of surprise as familiar faces began to pour into the street. Half-awake people stumbled onto the sidewalk, struggling with jackets and sobbing children.

Someone shrieked my name. "Philli!"

I turned to see my old friend Cami barreling towards me. She collided into me and nearly knocked us both to the ground. "You came back!"

I gripped her as she sobbed into my shoulder. "It's okay, you're going to be okay."

A ripple passed across the crowd. "Phil?" "Is that Smyrna's kid?" "It's Blue Fire!"

I looked up. The commotion on the street stilled as everyone turned to me.

Jayde touched my back. "Let them see you."

I disentangled myself from Cami and stepped out into the street. "Yes, it's me. You're not safe here anymore—but we're going to get you out. These soldiers are my friends." I nodded at Jayde. "Follow them and you'll be safe."

There was silence, and for a second, I thought they weren't going to obey me. Then Cami's brother Aid shoved his way through the crowd and came to stand beside me. "You came back for us," he said, his voice husky but bold.

I looked up into his face. "Of course I did. I couldn't leave you."

He smiled and held out a hand—then changed his mind and pulled me into a hug. I accepted it and felt the weight of responsibility crash into my shoulders. *I can't leave these people.*

Jayde clapped his hands. "You heard her! Move out!"

The noise on the street resumed, this time with purpose. I pushed Aid away. "Head towards the front gate. I'll meet you when you get there—I promise."

He nodded and grabbed Cami's hand.

I turned to Stanyard. He stood on the sidewalk, feet apart, staring straight ahead.

I followed his gaze. Several doors down, Mr. Dass stood on his top step, scanning the crowd in confusion.

I touched Stanyard's shoulder. "He needs you."

Stanyard sucked in more air than his lungs could hold and nodded. He turned to Mira, who stood a few feet away, watching us.

He held out his hand.

She stared at it for what felt like a cursed eternity. I held my breath and willed her to take it. *God, please, restore.*

Mira finally reached out and accepted the offer, grabbing his fingers loosely. Stanyard led the way and pulled her through the crowd towards their old house.

Mr. Dass spotted them. I couldn't see his expression in the dark, but I could read his body language—the jerk of surprise, the stiffened back, his hands gripping the railing.

Stanyard and Mira stopped on the sidewalk. If words were exchanged, I didn't hear them. I whispered in tongues under my breath.

The tension shattered as Mr. Dass shouted for his wife. I watched with grateful tears as Stanyard finally got the reunion he deserved: His father diving off the porch and crushing him in a hug. Even Mira accepted her father's embrace as he used both arms to gather his children to him.

I turned away—and came face to face with my old door.

There it was, House 79, right across the street from the Dasses'. All the curtains were drawn, and weeds stubbornly grew in the cracks on the sidewalk.

Jayde appeared beside me. He pressed a flashlight into my hand. "You've got two minutes before the lights come on. Hurry."

I nodded and ran up the steps.

The door wasn't locked. It creaked as I stepped inside. The musty air rushed up to greet me, stale but familiar. I flicked the flashlight on and panned it over the entryway tile—the same floor my mother died on.

I swallowed the thought and hurried into the living room. I scanned the flashlight over the furniture, searching for any belongings I could easily take with me. I knew there was nothing upstairs; Thames had sent all my personal effects to Mars. But surely there was something…

There. My flashlight landed on the digital picture frame hanging on the wall. Propping the flashlight on the coffee table, I ran over and grabbed the frame off the wall. It was wireless, so as soon as I touched it, the screen brightened to life, revealing my favorite picture of Daddy and me.

I gripped the frame. The picture had been taken before we moved into camp, and Daddy's eyes were still full of life and purpose. He was staring down at me as I wrapped my arms around his waist, my face scrunched in laughter and my long hair flowing in the wind. He smiled at me with all the love of a father—affection I'd never get again.

I hugged the frame to my chest, choking on waves of emotion. I didn't know whether to be sad or bitter or just plain angry—mad at everything that had been taken from me. My mom was gone. My dad was gone. I—Philadelphia—was gone. We could end the United and liberate the world, but the Smyrnas were never coming back.

Mira was right. I couldn't fix everything.

I knew what I needed to do. Turning around, I faced the living room—the worn couch where my family had shared so many tears and stolen moments of joy—and spoke into the darkness.

"Goodbye, Mama. I love you."

I sniffed and swallowed.

"Goodbye, Daddy. I'll miss you."

I choked on a sob. I stared at the ceiling and forced the last words out.

"I hope I make you proud."

Suddenly, the lights came on.

Tower's voice crackled over the radio. "Gate's open! Load out!"

Shouts echoed on the street. Wiping my eyes, I ran out the front door and left House 79 behind for good.

I stepped onto the porch to find the street nearly empty. Stanyard stood at the end of the block, flagging the last people around the corner. Jayde waited for me at the bottom of the steps.

"Smile for the camera." He gestured behind me.

I turned and saw the security camera on the light pole, its lens flickering as it rebooted.

"Want to leave a calling card?" John came around the corner of the house, shaking a can of spray paint in each hand.

"You brought spray paint?" Jayde exclaimed.

"We always come prepared to vandalize," Dowe returned.

John rattled the cans. "Pink or blue?" he asked me.

I grinned. "Blue," I said, and caught it as he tossed it at me.

Taking a step back, I studied my old house. Then I aimed the can and drew a jagged bolt of lightning across the front door.

"Blue Fire was here," I declared, then turned and stared straight into the camera, making sure the tattoo on my shoulder was visible.

Jayde nodded in approval. "All right, let's move out!" He jogged towards Stanyard, calling final instructions at his men.

I dropped the paint can and followed John and Dowe back to the wall. Orders ricocheted on the radio as each vehicle pulled out, carrying its precious cargo. *Oh Jesus—protect them!* I prayed.

"Race you!" John shouted at his partner, and they darted ahead of me.

A few yards behind them, I came around the corner to the last street—just in time to see Lieutenant Clint get up.

He moaned and rolled over. He pushed himself against a light pole and reached for his guns, cursing when he found them gone. He pulled out his radio and pressed the button.

"Stop!" I yelled, darting towards him.

He jerked his head around. I whipped the gun from my pocket. "Put it down!"

He let go of the button.

I stopped a few yards away and aimed the gun at his face. Muscle memory kicked in as I planted my feet apart, my hands steady even though I thought my heart was going to break a rib. "Put it down, or I shoot," I ordered.

He snorted. "Will you?"

I hesitated, my grip slacking.

"Blue Fire!" Jayde shouted from behind me.

Clint shook his head. "You won't. I know you, Philadelphia."

"Do you?" I hissed, taking another step forward.

He didn't flinch. "Your finger's not even on the trigger."

"Just shoot him!" Jayde called, still too far away to help me.

My eyes shifted from Clint's face to his uniform, with the shiny badge that represented the government that had tortured me for so long. I remembered the threats at gunpoint, the propagandizing at school, all the shouts and abuse as they told me over and over that I was worthless, broken, and unwanted.

My finger slid to the trigger, and I saw the light behind Clint's eyes change.

"Phil!" Stanyard shouted from somewhere in my peripheral.

I became aware of the weight of the gun in my hand as clarity rushed into my mind. Clint deserved to die—but without his radio, he was harmless. We'd be long gone before he could make it to the guard tower to call for help.

I adjusted my grip. "I'm not going to ask you again. Put. It. Down."

After a flicker of hesitation, he threw the radio on the pavement. It skidded towards me.

I kept the gun aimed. "Phone."

He grunted and fished it out of his pocket, tossing it at me.

I waited until it had spun to a stop on the pavement. Then I drew my foot back and stomped on both devices, crushing them.

I lowered the gun. "When you get back to headquarters, tell them Blue Fire sent you."

He didn't say anything. He just stared at me, eyes narrowed.

I turned and ran.

8

I didn't take a full breath until we were back at base.

As soon as I climbed into the SUV and slammed the door shut, the reality of what we'd just done collapsed on me—along with the reality of what I'd almost done. Stanyard rode with his family, so I was alone in the SUV with Lev and Jayde. Jayde barked directions into the radio as he raced through the alleys, but I didn't hear a word anyone was saying. I stared at the gun in my hands and felt the cold touch of the lethal metal on my fingertips.

You almost shot him in the face!

"Hey, you don't need that anymore," Lev muttered, followed by some words in Russian. He gingerly slid the weapon from my grasp and set the safety.

I stared down at my hands, so pale and shaky and streaked with substances I dare not identify, and wondered if they still belonged to me.

Lev pushed his googles back and pulled the handkerchief off his nose. "You good, boss?"

"I almost… I almost killed him," I whispered, afraid the words would kill me too as I spoke them.

"What?"

"I almost killed him. I almost killed him!" I shouted, as if the volume could force me to accept this new reality that I'd created.

"You should have," Jayde grunted, his eyes finding mine in the rearview mirror.

"But you didn't." The inflection in Lev's voice was somewhere between a statement and a question, his brow furrowed as he studied me.

Most of the vans dispersed across the city, taking the refugees to different drop-off points to avoid suspicion, but the Dasses and Cami and Aid's family were coming to base at my request. Tower had personally agreed to transport the Dasses, and Cami and Aid's family rode with John and Dowe.

As soon as we all arrived back at base, Cami barreled into me, gushing all over again. Her parents hugged me and then plied me with all the well-meaning adult questions I didn't have the energy to answer truthfully: *"Where have you been? What's going on? Where's your father?"*

I looked for Stanyard, but he was busy getting his family settled. So I let them have their privacy and took Cami and Aid up with me to the command floor, where we waited for the other teams to check in. We stood around the module with Jayde, Lev, and Tower, watching the screen. A map of the city with all the drop-off points was displayed on the monitor, while a police scanner tracked the ongoing state of emergency.

It didn't take long for our jailbreak to reach headquarters and send the government into high alert. Within an hour they had the highways closed down, traffic scanners set up at a dozen major intersections, and police out on every corner looking for suspicious vehicles.

The silence on the radio was cruel. I pinched my eyes shut and repeated my prophetic prayers over and over.

They're all going to make it. No one will get pulled over. Everyone will be safe—

And then, suddenly, the first team checked in.

Air rushed back into the room as the soldiers murmured gratefully. I opened my eyes and watched the first team's dot on the map turn green. *Thank you, Jesus.*

One by one, the other captains called in, until every last team was accounted for. I stared at the map, now splattered with green dots, and blinked away tears.

They all made it. We did it. We won.

Jayde stepped forward and offered me his hand. "Congratulations, Blue Fire. Mission accomplished."

The room erupted in applause. Cami squealed and hugged me. Lev laughed, his face crinkled in the largest smile I'd ever seen him wear.

I felt hands slide over my shoulders. I looked up into my uncle's face, his smile hidden under the shadow of his shaggy hair. "Now *that's* how you lead a revolution."

I scanned the room and watched as the soldiers exchanged hugs and high fives and tears. Someone started a military chant, and the whole room joined in, pumping their fists in time. I listened to the war cry reverberate through my bones and finally admitted the truth.

This is where you belong.

*

Stanyard met me in the cafeteria when I stumbled down for breakfast the next morning.

"There you are," he said, turning and gesturing to the open bench beside him.

I wanted to say the same thing; I hadn't seen him or Mira since we got back to base last night. I joined him at the table, setting my backpack down on the floor, and accepted the mug of black coffee he had ready for me. I smiled at the rippling brown liquid. "Were you waiting for me?"

"Always," he said, and grinned. "How are you feeling?"

I arched my back. "Sore," I admitted. The stiffness hadn't hit me until this morning, when the adrenaline finally dried up.

He hesitated, then gently reached over and rubbed my back. When I didn't shy away, he pressed harder, grinding his knuckles in between my shoulder blades. I laid my forehead on my arms and flopped out on the table with a relieved sigh. I let him work, wondering, not for the first time, when he'd become so kind—or if he'd always been this nice, and I just never noticed.

I stiffened and sat up when I remembered what else had transpired yesterday. "But what about you? How did it…?"

"Ask me when I've had more sleep." He snorted and lowered his hand. "I don't think any of us slept more than a couple hours. It's a lot for Mom and Dad to take in."

Of course it was, but that wasn't what I was asking. "Did you and your dad have time to talk?"

He nodded, staring at the stain in the bottom of his empty mug.

I laid my hand on his knee. "And?"

His shoulders heaved as he took a deep breath. "I apologized. And… so did he."

I gripped his leg, my heart bursting with praise.

He looked up and stared at the wall, brow furrowed as if he was still trying to comprehend his new reality. "Now we have to figure out how to live with each other again."

I smiled in spite of myself. "And what about Mira?" I dared to ask.

He tapped the handle of his coffee mug. "She needs more time."

And Jesus, I thought but didn't add.

"You were right about one thing, though."

I looked up at him. "Yeah?"

He turned to meet my eyes. "I have to forgive myself first."

I studied the creases around the corners of his mouth and wondered if he hadn't quite accomplished that yet. "I forgive you," I reminded him. "And… I'm proud of you."

He started slightly, for a brief moment pulling back. Then he leaned towards me. "Thank you," he whispered, his eyes flickering with an expression I understood but dare not put words to.

I stared at him, wanting for all the world to say *yes* to the unspoken question between us. Before I could second guess what I was doing, I slid down the bench and laid my head on his shoulder.

He relaxed into me, slowly, as if he were afraid he'd displace me. His hand found mine beneath the table.

I closed my eyes and had just found my peace when Stanyard's phone buzzed.

He stiffened but made no move to pick it up. It pulsed three more times, vibrating irritatingly against the metal table.

I groaned and lifted my head. "If that's Jayde…" *I'll fire him.*

Stanyard sighed and grabbed the device, flipping it over to read the screen. His brow scrunched. "It's Nic."

I sat up straight. "What?"

He flipped through the notifications. "He's mad you didn't check in last night."

I hadn't even looked at my tablet last night when I'd stopped in at the Vons'—I'd had more important things to do. "And he's texting *you* about that?"

Stanyard shrugged. "He's also asking if you saw the news."

"I try not to. Why?" But as soon as I said it, I knew what had happened.

I hadn't told Nic what we were doing last night. There hadn't been time, and this was definitely a situation where it would be better to ask for forgiveness than permission—or, better yet, not tell him at all. But apparently the media had done my job for me.

The phone buzzed again. "He's asking me to call him."

"Don't," I said emphatically, standing up and grabbing my backpack.

"Or, never mind, I guess he's calling me." The phone trilled, and Stanyard answered it before I could stop him. "Hello?"

"Where is she?" Nic demanded, voice rigid with anger.

My palms started to sweat as my fight-or-flight response kicked in, but I willed it back. This didn't involve him, and I wasn't going to let him bully me this time. I did what was right.

Stanyard held the phone away from his ear and looked up at me. "She's right here."

"Of course she is." Nic sighed, and I pictured him aggressively rubbing a hand across his mustache. "I hope you're leaving room for Jesus."

Stanyard flushed red. "Huh?"

"Never mind. Put her on."

Stanyard offered the phone to me. I didn't take it.

"Philadelphia," Nic barked, "don't be a coward."

I snatched the device and walked a few feet away. "Don't be a jerk."

"I'll think about it. Who signed the parental waiver?"

"What?" I sighed, and hoped he wouldn't keep beating around the bush. I knew he was upset, but it would be a lot easier to deal with if he'd just be honest with me.

"Your tattoo. Who signed the parental waiver? Because I sure didn't."

"It's temporary," I admitted. Why was I humoring him? It really wasn't any of his business.

"That's a relief, because it's ugly."

My face burned as his words stung a part of my soul I didn't realize he had access to. *It's not ugly... I'm not ugly, am I?* I glanced down at what was left of the drawing on my shoulder.

Stanyard stood up and waited by the table, watching me.

"Anyway," Nic continued, his voice a starched façade of calm, "are you aware, Miss Smyrna, of how insufferably moronic you've been the last twenty-four hours, or do I need to explain it to you?"

My hand tightened around the phone. If he wanted to take cheap shots, two could play that game. "Why don't you explain it to me, Dr. Von Nieuwenhuyse? Enlighten me with your three PhDs."

I knew he hated his full name, and I could tell by the shift in his tone that I'd hurt him where he hurt me. "Watch your attitude, young lady."

"I learned from the best," I hissed.

He couldn't deny it, so he ignored it. "All right then, I hope you're taking notes, because there will be a quiz in the morning. First of all, thanks to your little outing last night, your name and image are now plastered all over the news—again."

That was, of course, the idea, but I daren't tell him that. "They already knew my name."

"Yes, well, now they have live footage proving you're in town, and they have visual descriptions of several of your 'friends.' What in the world were you thinking?"

The anger in his voice cracked, making room for genuine fear. I heard the desperation in his words and remembered why we were having this conversation. Nic was a jerk, yes, but he really did care about me.

"Nic." I took several breaths to regulate the tone of my voice. "That was my camp. Those were my old neighbors."

"'Old' should be the operative word there."

"No, Nic, listen." I tried to cram a brick in the door while it was open. "They were going to deport them."

He was silent.

I looked to Stanyard for support as I continued. "We intercepted orders from the regional office. They were all going to be deported to a labor camp in China in the morning. They… weren't coming back."

"I know." Nic sighed, but I couldn't tell if the gesture was a concession or not.

I swallowed and tried to force my heart out through my words, desperate for him to see my side. "They did it because of me, Nic. I just found out that they've been interrogating everyone I knew, trying to get to me."

"And that's exactly why you should have left it alone."

"What?"

His voice hardened again, each syllable thick with disappointment. "They baited you, Phil, and you played right into their hand. You should have walked away."

I'm not sure which upset me more: his disapproval or the horror of what he was suggesting. "You think I should have let them get deported?"

"It's what I would have done," he stated with absolutely no remorse at all, and in that moment, I remembered why he had once been the villain.

"Nic!" I cried. "They would have been *killed*!"

"It would have been their own fault," he stated.

Stanyard stiffened. Nic blathered on with no regard for the grave he was digging for himself. "Last I checked, the jewelry counter at the store has more security than those containment camps. If they wanted to break out, they would have done so before now."

I didn't want to think about the fact that, had it not been for Nic and the Red Rain fiasco, *I* would still be in that camp.

"You should have left it alone, Phil," Nic repeated, his voice grave. "These people that you're playing with—the officials in Beijing—they're out of your league. Trust me, I know. You need to walk away while you still can."

No. I was tired of turning a blind eye while the government destroyed people's lives. The whole reason the world was in this mess was because people had walked away, content to hibernate in their cocoon of security while freedom fell. That's what Nic had done. He'd built his castle on Mars and never looked back.

I wouldn't make the same mistake.

"I'm sorry I'm not more like you," I spat, withdrawing the affection from my voice.

"Well, let me know how that works out for you," his tone tightened in kind, "because you just made things so much worse."

My anger evaporated as my heart dropped to my stomach. I shared a panicked glance with Stanyard. "What do you mean?"

"Oh, you haven't heard? Maybe you should go turn on the TV, 'Blue Fire,'" he threatened. "You may have won a battle last night, but you're about to lose a war."

I hung up on him and started running.

9

We raced up to the command floor, paging Jayde as we went. A few bored guards were lounging around the controls when we arrived. Mira leaned against the dashboard, chatting with one of them.

She straightened when we entered. "What's wrong with you?" She gave me a once-over, her eyes distinctly avoiding Stanyard's.

I brushed past her. "Turn on the news."

"Why?"

One of the guards obeyed me without question, his fingers flying across a control pad. I saw the screen in front of him light up, the image dancing across the reflection on his glasses. He uttered something that could have been taken as either a prayer or an oath.

I gripped the dashboard. "Put it on the screen."

The door whooshed open and Jayde walked in just as the monitor above our heads flickered on, displaying the morning newscast. Clips of security footage from last night's raid played in the background, superimposed with the panicked words

Breaking News. I watched as an eerily high-definition, black-and-white version of myself spraypainted a lightning bolt on the door of my old home.

Then I looked down at the ticker. I watched the words roll past, spelling out the doomed headline:

BEIJING OFFICIALS VOTE TO RESTRUCTURE ASSIMILATION ASSISTANCE PROGRAM

Stanyard muttered in tongues. I couldn't find anything to say as I listened to a plastic anchorwoman read off her tablet.

"Officials say the instigator behind last night's violent demonstration is Philadelphia Smyrna, a runaway from a Boston remedial home."

"'Remedial home'? How charming," Stanyard muttered.

To reinforce the veneer of benevolence, they popped up a quaint picture of me coloring with chalk on the sidewalk at camp. It was a grainy photo, clearly ripped from a security camera and zoomed in to crop out the watchtower and concrete fence in the background.

I remembered that day; it was not long after we'd been taken into camp, and I was only eleven or twelve. Dad had smuggled some sidewalk chalk home from work, and I'd amused myself for a week, drawing castles and unicorns to transport myself somewhere else.

I'd shared my treasure with Mira. I looked up at her where she stood across the room and wondered if she remembered, but if she did, it wasn't a pleasant memory. She was frowning at the screen, her arms crossed.

The anchorwoman continued narrating.

"Smyrna went missing shortly after being removed from a high school special ed program. People close to the suspect claim she was a well-adjusted girl before being forced to graduate early, leading many to blame the school system."

They cut to a clip of my homeroom teacher. *"She was an excellent student,"* he crooned, which was the exact opposite of what he'd always told me. *"Eager to learn, very responsive to redirection. She was really trying, but the system was designed for her to fail."*

"That's because I wanted to fail," I snorted, but the laugh stopped in my throat, like it was food I couldn't swallow. This wasn't funny—it was terrifying.

"Psychological experts say Smyrna's actions display classic signs of conduct disorder and borderline personality disorder. And there's mounting scientific evidence that both of these disorders can be caused by conditions in the remedial homes."

The screen flashed to carefully curated clips from my streams—the ones that looked shaky, amateur, and childish. The ones that made me look like a scared teenager with a laptop.

"This young woman should have been diagnosed years ago," some random guy with a bunch of letters after his name droned. *"It's been clinically proven that these 'homes' are actually preventing kids from rejoining society."*

So this was how they were going to cover their mess: By making me sound sick and diseased, like a lab rat. But in some disgusting way, they were right. The camps did turn me into the monster they thought I was. I did what I did because of the camps—because I didn't want anyone else to suffer like I did.

Suddenly, Asia appeared on the screen.

She stood behind a podium emblazoned with the United seal, cameras flashing in the background. *"This 'rebellion' is clearly a troubled young woman's cry for help. Children like her need our aid, not our punishment..."*

"That's her!" I lurched back and pointed. "That's Asia, the woman who gave me the code."

A murmur rippled around the room. Jayde stepped up beside me and swore. "Then you're in big trouble."

I looked at him. "What?"

He pointed to the corner where Asia's real name was displayed:

MONG SHI MIN TAI, COUNCILOR

The commotion in the room escalated. My mind struggled to peg the familiar surname, and when it finally did, my heart stopped.

Oh God, no.

I yanked my backpack off my shoulders and struggled with the zipper. I grabbed the invitation and ripped it out of the envelope, holding the cursed calligraphy up to the light.

HIS EXCELLENCE GENERAL SECRETARY MONG

The room faded as I remembered everything they'd taught us in school. Asia was the daughter of the General Secretary, the highest-ranking official in the United government.

And she knew exactly who I was, dual identities and all.

Jayde grabbed his radio and yelled for Tower, then started shouting orders to his men. I turned my focus back to Asia, squinting at the video and trying to read the motivation behind her expression. What was she doing? My rebellion threatened her government, her position in society. She should have been the first one to turn me in, but she hadn't. What did she want?

I tuned into her words as the video kept rolling.

"We are failing our children. None of this would have happened if the state had placed Philadelphia in a loving home instead of locking her behind bars. And now we have officials calling for her execution? Please, I'm begging my friends in Washington: Let this poor child come home."

She looked up and smiled benevolently at the camera, as if she knew I was watching. I took an instinctive step back. She wanted me to come home. She still wanted me to become Andromeda, to accept a life of affluence and live like one of them, and she would move heaven, earth, and hell until that was the only choice I had.

But why? Why was I so important to her? For that matter, why had I been so important to Thames? He had picked me out long before my dad had created Red Rain. I'd been a pawn in the end, but that's not how it had started. He had chosen me. Why?

Stanyard touched my elbow, his eyes narrowed, searching for answers to the same questions. I gripped his hand as the anchorwoman appeared on the screen again.

"These developments have experts all across the globe calling for reform of the reassimilation program. In an emergency session early this morning, Beijing officials voted almost unanimously to close the North American branch of the program and relocate detainees to compounds in China."

The room devolved into a hurricane of curses and shouts of rage. Stanyard turned away from me and rammed his fist into the nearest desk. Lev muttered in Russian. Even Jayde went silent, his face pale and pinched as he gripped the dashboard.

Mira moved beside me. "Look what you've done," she hissed.

I slapped my hands over my ears as Nic's accusations came ricocheting back.

You may have won a battle last night, but you're about to lose a war.

I could barely hear the recording as another United official came on the screen and praised the decision.

"This debacle clearly demonstrates the inefficiencies of the North American system. It is critical that these people are transferred to a stable environment before more lives are lost. We can assure you that the detainees will receive the finest medical care and psychological screening..."

The roar from the soldiers drowned him out. The room was spinning, spinning as I dropped the invitation and staggered for any handhold, finding only the dashboard. I braced myself against the controls and fought alternating waves of nausea, tears, and guilt.

You should have stayed on Mars, sweetheart.

No. I slammed my palm down on the control panel, freezing the stream. This can't be how it ends. I'd come too far, survived too many miracles, for this to all be a mistake. I wasn't going to give up, not this time.

God had brought me to this point, and I wasn't going back to Mars until I found out why.

"No," I said again, this time aloud. I whipped around and repeated myself, strong enough to be heard. "No."

The commotion stilled as everyone shifted to look at me. I accepted the responsibility and straightened. "We can't let this happen—*I* can't let this happen."

I am Blue Fire.

"And what are you going to do about it?" Mira threw up her hands. "Liberate the camps one by one and hide people in the basement? You can't fix this, Phil. The only reason this is happening is because *you* felt the need to show off."

"Mira," Stanyard hissed, an unfamiliar anger rising in his eyes.

"No, no," I muttered, mostly to myself, giving my mind time to catch up. She was right, of course—we couldn't save all those people, not like that. But there had to be something else I could do. We'd managed to rally an army just with one video; surely that wasn't for nothing.

I took a step back, as if the motion could help me see in another dimension, and my foot slipped on the invitation. I stared at the gilded lettering peeking out from beneath my scuffed shoe and remembered the handwritten note on the back of the envelope.

YOU'RE STILL INVITED –ASIA

I bent and picked up the card, and suddenly, I understood why God had chosen me.

I looked up at the group. "Let me talk to her."

"Who?" Stanyard demanded, instantly suspicious.

"Asia—Councilor Mong. She loves me. She's been trying to be friends since we met—and she can fix this. Maybe if I talk to her, or go to the party, she will—"

"What party?" Jayde interrupted.

I shoved the invitation at him. I paced a tight circle around the middle of the floor, trying to anchor my thoughts. I had no idea what I would say or how I would approach her, but I knew this was what I was supposed to do. *This* was why—this was why Thames had taken an interest in me. This was why Asia had befriended me. This was why I was a Nolan.

I realized the room had gone silent. I looked up at Jayde. He was frowning at the invitation, eyes dark and cold.

"Everyone out," he ordered. "I need to talk to Blue Fire."

10

After a flicker of hesitation, the soldiers obeyed him, filing out of the room.

Lev and Stanyard held back. Lev cast a questioning glare up at Jayde and rattled off something in Russian that apparently Jayde understood.

Jayde shook his head. "I said everyone."

Lev turned and hurried out. Stanyard frowned, planted his feet apart, and didn't move.

Jayde tensed, but Mira intercepted. She grabbed her brother's shoulder and steered him towards the door. With a final glance back at me, Stanyard relented.

Jayde waited until the door had shut behind them. Then he walked over to the dashboard and pressed down on a key. "Blackout," he declared into the empty room.

With a dying whir of electricity, all the computers in the room shut off. The dashboard grew cold as the buttons stopped flickering, and the monitor went black, plunging the room into near darkness. The only light left in the room came from the blinking sensors on the wall of servers.

I groped for a handhold. "Jayde…"

I heard his boots clumping on the floor, and then a lone desk lamp flickered on. He stood there, his back to me, holding the invitation under the yellow light.

"Why didn't you tell me about this sooner?"

It was none of your business would have been the correct answer, but I was quickly realizing that, as Blue Fire, everything that happened to me was someone else's business.

"I didn't think it was important," I settled for, and up until moments ago, it hadn't been.

"Phil…" He turned and shook the paper at me. "Do you understand what this is an invitation for?"

"Yeah, some state dinner." Asia had specifically called it a "boring" state dinner.

"Not just any state dinner. *The* state dinner. This is the most prestigious government event of the year. Don't you remember seeing it on the news?"

I thought we'd established today that I didn't watch the news, but even if I had, a state dinner wasn't something I would have paid attention to. Watching rich people crossbreed at parties was the exact opposite of entertaining.

"Only the most elite get invited. That's how they decide who's in and who's out for the next round of government commissions." Jayde paced, his face passing in and out of shadow. "Everyone who attends gets to meet the General Secretary, and it's all televised on live TV."

And I'm one of those elite. I tried and failed to grasp the complexity of that revelation.

"If I had realized that's what this woman was inviting you to when you met…" Jayde stood still and blinked, recalibrating his reality around a dimension of *what-ifs*. He shook his head and turned towards me. "Phil, if you go, you'll get to meet the General face-to-face."

That sounded like a reason why I should *not* go. The General Secretary was the last person I wanted to get a close look at me.

Asia may know who I was, but logical deduction assumed her father did not. If he did, I wouldn't still be breathing.

Jayde studied me, watching to see if I was tracking the implications. When I didn't produce the desired reaction, he gestured behind me. "Sit down."

I glanced at the nearby desk chair. "Why?" I demanded, and tried to figure out why that command was vaguely threatening.

"Please," was all he said.

I refused.

He inhaled through his nose and pinched his eyes shut. "This is going to be very difficult for you to hear, but I need you to listen carefully." He opened his eyes. "I know how we can win this war."

"How?" I said, knowing full well that I didn't want the answer.

He spoke slowly, each word metered like the steady bang of a drum. "You need to accept the invitation," he held it out, "meet the General, and kill him."

"What?" I breathed. I'd heard him the first time. I just didn't want to accept it.

He repeated himself even more slowly. "You will go to the party, meet the General, and assassinate him."

No, I started to say, but the word died as soon as I formed it. *I can't.*

"You can," he countered my thoughts. "It's just like Asia said—you're a Nolan. You're one of them. And if your family is as famous as she makes them sound, the General will definitely want to meet you and shake your hand."

"But Thames—" Mr. Nolan had fallen out of grace with the United, and he'd decided he'd rather die than deal with the consequences. And his crimes were petty compared to mine. Surely his sins had tainted the family name.

"Asia can take care of that," Jayde declared without even the slightest hesitation. "She already has. Do you think you would have gotten this invitation if they suspected Andromeda?"

I remembered how Asia had so sweetly offered to clear Mrs. Nolan's file and realized he was right. If the Nolans were being penalized for their involvement in Red Rain, I would have heard about it by now. Asia had made the whole thing go away.

Perhaps, I recognized for the first time, because she had been in charge all along.

"You can do this," Jayde repeated, sealing the verdict while there was nowhere for me to run. "You can get close enough to him. Andromeda can."

He was right. Andromeda could do this.

But that didn't mean Philadelphia would.

"I won't," I said, and wished my voice had come out stronger, more convicted.

"You have to."

He stepped forward. I stumbled back, tripping over my backpack and spilling the contents on the floor. I heard a makeup tube roll away, thudding softly into a cabinet across the room.

He stopped on the edge of the light from the desk lamp. "This is how we end this, Phil. This is how we end the United."

"But Operation Blue Fire…" *That* was the plan. To revolt, to stand up together, to raise our voice and tell the government that we would not surrender. No one had to die for that plan to work. No one had to kill.

Jayde shook his head. "Operation Blue Fire will break the system, but it won't end it. No matter how many citizens join us, the United will still control the government. They're going to have their strongholds, and we'll have to fight them tooth and nail for control. It will be all-out war, Phil. Do you know what war means?"

Bloodshed. Death. Destruction.

I knew that. I knew the operation could lead to war; I'd known that this whole time. I hoped—and prayed—that things would go another way, that there would be enough resistance and the system would collapse on itself without the need for outright war. But war was always a possibility, and it was a sacrifice we were willing to make.

Was it possible that I could prevent war entirely?

"If you take out the General, it will throw the government into chaos." Jayde gestured in the air like he was drawing a battle plan on a map. "They'll be scrambling to replace him—and that's when we strike. That's when we launch Operation Blue Fire."

I wanted to refute him. I wanted to reject his plan and point out the flaws in his logic—but there were none.

"If we strike while they're weak, we can destroy the whole system. We can remove the government and build a new one."

Jayde's voice reached a fever pitch, but in my head, he sounded distant and small. There were dozens of questions I should be asking: *How are we going to get rid of the rest of the officials? Who will replace them? What kind of government will we build?* But I couldn't process any of that. All those hypothetical realities slipped through my fingers like sand as I choked on the bitter truth that underpinned them all.

You have to kill a man.

"You're the only one who can do it, Phil. No one else can get close enough. They won't let me anywhere near him—they don't know me. But they know you."

I finally took Jayde's advice and collapsed in the chair behind me. I heard rather than felt my breathing turn fast and shallow, became aware of the thrumming of my pulse as I gripped the arms of the chair. "I—I can't," I cried, but the word came out as a gasp, like I was drowning and couldn't keep my head above water.

"Yes, you can. I'll help you. We'll figure out a way to make it quick and bloodless. You won't be able to come at him with a traditional weapon—you're not going to have to stab him to death or anything."

Was that supposed to make it any better? "No, I can't!" I forced the words out with resolve, even though I was losing feeling in my hands and face.

"Phil—"

"I won't!"

The declaration echoed between us, drawing a line I wouldn't cross. Jayde stopped and waited until the silence returned. "Why not?" he asked finally, the question unnervingly calm.

"Because it's wrong," I answered reflexively. *Thou shalt not kill.*

"How is it any different than what you're already doing?"

I'm not murdering anyone.

He scoffed, crossing his arms over his bulky chest. "You signed up for this, Phil. When you agreed to be Blue Fire, you agreed to lead a revolution. You may not be on the front lines, but it's still war. If you don't pull the trigger, someone else will."

"So let them!" I screeched. *Anyone but me.*

"But if you do it, you can save so many lives," he pleaded, his voice softening again. "You can end this war before it starts."

I looked away. Every nerve in my body was screaming in refusal, but I couldn't find the words. Everything I could think to say felt weak, inadequate. Cowardly.

Jayde resorted to begging. "Phil, please. You have to be the one. I can't—" He stepped towards me, and his boot crunched on something. He bent to pick it up, rolling it over in his fingers. I couldn't see what it was in the shadows.

When he spoke again, his voice was soft, a cool whisper. "What if this is the reason you're here?"

I looked up at him and waited.

"You said yourself—Asia loves you. The Nolans chose you. Why?"

I wish I knew.

Jayde walked over and dropped down on one knee in front of me. "You're one of them now—but you're also Philadelphia. You're Blue Fire. You're the only one with a foot in both worlds."

He took my hand and gently spread my fingers. He pressed something cold and metallic into my palm.

I could tell what it was by the shape: the star of David pin Lev had given me. I stared at it as it glinted faintly in the darkness.

For such a time as this.

Jayde closed my fingers around the pin and gripped my fist. "This is why you're here, Phil. No one else can do this but you. Will you help me? Will you help me save the world?"

*

I closed the door to Cea's bedroom and sagged against it, relieved to finally be alone. Mr. Von had exacted vengeance on me for skipping out on dinner the last two nights and bullied me into watching six episodes of his current show. My mind was numb, and I was exhausted from the fake laughter—both the TV's and my own. It was nearly eleven o'clock before he finally let me escape.

I could only hope it wasn't too late to make a call.

I walked over to the nightstand and picked up the jewelry box Asia had given me. I opened the blue velvet case and fingered the single strand of pearls. Asia had claimed it was an "early birthday gift," and at the time, the gesture had seemed strange, unwelcome. Now, I was grateful for the gift. In one week, I would have an occasion to wear pearls.

Underneath the necklace was tucked Asia's calling card. I slid it out and ran my thumb over the gilded embossing. She'd said I could call anytime I needed anything. I was about to find out if she was telling the truth.

Sinking down on the edge of the bed, I took my tablet off the charger. There were several unread messages from both Nic and Stanyard, but I cleared the notifications and ignored them. If I didn't do this now, I'd lose my nerve.

I brought up the call screen and dialed Asia's number. She picked up after one ring.

"Andromeda!" she crooned into the phone, sounding wide awake. Her controlled Mandarin accent made her voice warm but spicy, like ginger. "It's so good to hear from you."

"Hi," I managed, but the word stuck in my throat.

Am I really doing this?

She latched onto my fear like a wolf. "What's wrong? Are you in danger? Do you need anything?"

I took three deep breaths through my nose and remembered what Jayde had said. *"Act frightened, like you've seen the light,"* he'd coached. *"If she asks, tell her you heard the news and realized you made a mistake. She won't question your change of heart—after all, that's what she wants."*

I swallowed and didn't try to suppress the stutter in my voice. "I—there's something I need to ask you."

"Yes?" she said, the question eager, too eager.

I pinched my eyes shut and squeezed out one last desperate prayer.

This is why you're here.

I opened my eyes and looked down at the screen. "Is it too late to RSVP to my birthday party?"

11

"This is going to hurt a lot."

"I know," I said, and hoped the pain medication Jayde had given me was working.

It was the next morning, and we were in the lab above Andes's shop. For the second time in so many months, I found myself strapped into the laser-guided surgery machine used to alter fingerprints.

Only this time, I wouldn't be changing my identity. This time, Andes would be weaving a network of wires and circuitry beneath the skin of my right hand, building a computer in my palm.

Andes snapped a magnifier over his right eye and blinked until it autofocused. Then he used tweezers to pick up a filament of wire, no thicker than a hair's breadth, and feed it into the machine.

"Brace yourself, lass," he warned, and lowered the needle into my thumb.

I shuddered. Whatever substance Jayde had given me was taking the edge off, but it didn't dull the horrifying feeling of the cold wire sliding into my skin. It was like a parasite, infesting me and turning me into a bomb.

That's what I was now: a walking weapon.

Jayde laid his warm hand on my shoulder, grounding me. "You're doing the right thing."

I nodded, not trusting my voice. He was right—he had to be. This is why I had been given all this privilege. This is why Thames had chosen me. This is why I was Andromeda Nolan.

I repeated that to myself over and over as Andes labored. It took an agonizing two hours, during which I cried out in pain more than once, before he was finally ready to install the motherboard.

Andes picked up the microscopic battery and held it close to the magnifier, his brow creased like a ravine. "What do you need this much power for, lass?"

I swallowed. I couldn't answer him truthfully.

I need that much power to kill.

The hardware was fairly simple. The computer would be programmed to deliver an electromagnetic pulse that would stop the heart and send the victim into cardiac arrest. Quick, bloodless, and irreversible.

All it needed was a microchip programmed to react to the General Secretary's DNA.

Andes arranged the battery on a sterile tray along with the other components of the motherboard. "I think you're missing some programming," he said. He directed the implied question at Jayde.

"It will be installed later," was all Jayde said, voice even.

Andes shifted his gaze back to me. He squinted, his right eye unnaturally large and bulbous behind the lens of the magnifier.

Please don't ask questions, I silently begged. Operation Thunderbird was a blackout mission. I couldn't even tell Stanyard.

Andes didn't ask for details, perhaps because he knew they wouldn't change anything. "Is this what you want, lass?"

I almost laughed. Maybe I should have; maybe the sound would have relieved some of the pain in my heart. No, this wasn't what I wanted. The last thing I wanted to do was kill.

But it was necessary.

I took a deep breath. "Do it."

Jayde squeezed my shoulder.

An eternity later, Andes finally released me from the machine. I stumbled out of the chair. My entire body was numb. My head pulsed with the reality of what I'd just done, what I'd just become. I rubbed my palm, trying to feel the wires and convince myself that this was real, but it was like my fingers weren't even there.

"How much?" Jayde grunted.

Andes put his hands up. "On the house. Consider it my investment in the new world."

I offered him a dizzy smile.

He stood up and grasped my shoulder, steadying me. "*Thig ar latha*, Thunderbird."

I used his brawny arm to pull myself upright. "There is one thing you can do for me."

He arched an eyebrow.

I rolled my sleeve up, baring my right shoulder. "I need a tattoo."

*

"I swear that hurt worse than the implant."

Jayde chuckled as he put the SUV in park. "You're the one who wanted it."

"Well, it's definitely my last." I gingerly rubbed the bandage that covered my new ink. For such a small design, it had taken almost thirty minutes of repetitive stabbing to create. I had been in complete agony the entire time; the pain medication had worn off, apparently. How people like Andes could willingly cover themselves in tattoos was beyond me.

"Hey." Jayde shut off the engine and swiveled to face me. "Thank you."

I tried not to look surprised, but my eyebrows had a mind of their own. "That's a new one coming from you."

He snorted. "I know. I don't say it often enough. But I couldn't do this without you."

"Do you really mean that?" I blurted with more transparency than I'd intended. Jayde was always telling me I was irreplaceable, but was it true? Nic thought the rebellion didn't need me. Even Stanyard thought I should just go home.

Jayde nodded. "I always have. I've always believed in you."

I eyed him, not sure I trusted this mushy and emotional version of Jayde.

"What?" he returned with an expression that was cross between amused and annoyed. "Do you think I would have tracked you across the entire Boston metropolitan area if you could be replaced?"

I rolled my eyes. "Way to kill the moment."

"Sorry." He laughed. "But think about it. If anyone else could have done it, don't you think I would have tried that before now? But I knew you were the one. That's why I put all my money on you."

I glanced at him out of the corner of my eye. "Was it a good investment?"

He leaned back in his seat and studied me. "You really don't see it, do you? You really don't understand what you've done."

I felt heat rising in my palms and up the back of my neck, but it wasn't a scary feeling.

"Phil, we've been trying for *years* to build what you've created in a matter of months. Ever since your dad..." He hesitated, chewing on his anger until he'd reduced it to a piece we could both swallow. "Ever since the original Operation Blue Fire failed, we've been trying to rally the people, but they've been too scared, too divided, too… distracted."

I thought back to all the years I'd spent willingly languishing in prison and realized he was right.

He drummed his finger on the steering wheel. "You're the first person I've met who wasn't scared."

"But that's not true. I am scared," I admitted, mostly to myself. *I'm terrified.*

His vivid green eyes found mine again. "Maybe. But you never let it stop you."

I stared down at my palm, still flushed and tender from the procedure. All my life I'd been afraid of something or someone, and I was still afraid now. I was afraid of the government, I was afraid of Asia, I was afraid of what would happen if someone found out what we were doing.

And, in a cold cruelty, I was afraid of what would happen if I succeeded.

I'd always been afraid, but somewhere in the halls of Wing 74, I'd found my courage. When I flipped over that table of chemicals, I'd made the decision that fear wouldn't make my choices for me. I could fight through the fear because I knew I was doing the right thing.

And because I knew Who was with me.

Jayde opened the car door. "There will always be something to be afraid of. There will always be someone bigger and scarier telling you what to do. The question is if you're going to obey."

He got out and slammed the door. I hesitated with my fingers clenched around the handle.

We must obey God rather than man.

I swallowed a prayer and opened the door.

"Where in the world have you been?"

I looked up to see Stanyard planted in the parking lot. His cheeks were flushed and his hair was disheveled, a sure sign he'd spent the morning pacing.

I cringed with embarrassment. I hadn't told Stanyard what we were doing; I'd hardly talked to him at all in the past twenty-four hours. Jayde and I had been behind closed doors all yesterday afternoon, working out the mission details and making calls. He'd taken me home, and then, to add insult to injury, he'd picked me up this morning and taken me straight to Andes's.

I'd responded to Stanyard's texts briefly last night to let him know I was okay, but almost everything I told him was a lie. I couldn't tell him what I was really doing, so all I could do was make up platitudes that sounded fake and disinterested. I'd muted the app and turned my tablet off before he could come online and try to call me.

I hated lying to him. I would almost rather not talk to him at all.

Unfortunately, it was a lot harder to avoid him in person.

"What were you doing this morning?" he repeated when I didn't answer his interrogation fast enough. "You didn't even respond to my texts."

I heard the hurt seeping through the anger in his voice and looked away. "I had an appointment."

"For what?" He paused and answered his own question. "You got a *tattoo*?"

He sounded absolutely horrified. No, worse than that—he sounded *ashamed*. He sounded just like Nic.

I slid my hand over my bandage.

"Dude, back off." Jayde stepped forward, shielding me. "It's none of your business."

Stanyard took that as an invitation to rear himself to his full height. "Yes, it is."

Jayde simply eyed him over the edge of his nose like he was a bug to be squashed. "How so?"

"She's my friend," Stanyard returned. The statement was incredulous, but the look he cast me was anything but.

Don't you still trust me?

I do, I wanted to answer him. *But I can't. Not with this.*

Jayde spared me the misery of another lie. "Yeah, well everyone in this building is her friend, so lay off it," he grunted. "This doesn't concern you. C'mon, Phil."

He started across the parking lot, and I ran to keep up with his long strides. I threw a glance over my shoulder and prepared to mouth an *I'm sorry* at Stanyard.

I changed my mind when I saw the anger burning on his face.

Jayde led us into the building and straight to the elevator. "What are we doing?" I asked as the doors closed.

"You have training to do."

All the camaraderie he'd generated with his motivational speech evaporated. I groaned. "I just spent four hours getting stabbed by needles, and now you want me to train?"

He didn't even gratify that with a response. We descended to the basement and walked to a room I knew all too well: the gun range.

My hands cramped at the very sight of the room. "Jayde, what's the point? I'm not going to need a gun at the party." I probably wouldn't have a gun on me the entire trip; I'm sure Asia's security was better than that.

"This isn't about your aim." He walked up to the control panel and pressed his thumb to the keypad. With a beep, all the dangling targets retracted back into the wall.

He swiped his fingers on the screen, and suddenly, the entire room went dark. With a crackle of electricity, a gridwork of purple laser light lit up, turning the room into a giant piece of graph paper. Jayde keyed in more commands, and the light began to congregate in the middle of the room, focusing until it formed the rough shape of a human. The figure was expressionless, like a mannequin.

"Here, put this on." Jayde held out a visor. It was thick and shiny but surprisingly light. I gingerly slid it over my eyes and turned to face the gun range. I couldn't see the laser light anymore. Instead, I could see a man.

He was stiff and robotic, his eyes refusing to blink, but he looked uncomfortably real. His skin was tan and marked with believable scratches and bruises. His clothes were soft, fabric rippling as he breathed in and out.

And his eyes. They were blue. Such a bright, bright blue.

"Earplugs," Jayde said from somewhere on my left. I turned, and he appeared in the viewscreen, his whole body highlighted in an angry red.

I lurched back. "Why are you red?" I took the earbuds he handed to me and popped them in.

His voice came through the plugs slightly warped. "Because you don't want to shoot me." He grabbed my wrist and forced a gun into my palm.

The balance of the room swung upside down as I realized what he was proposing. I looked back at the eerie hologram in the middle of the range. "Jayde, I—"

He didn't patronize me this time. "You have to. Phil, I'm not going to sugarcoat it. You're going to Beijing, and you're going to kill a man. And we both know what happened the last time you needed to kill someone."

Images of Lieutenant Clint lying on the concrete flashed through my mind. "But he didn't have to die."

"Debatable," Jayde muttered, "but this time, there's no other option. Either you kill the General, or everyone in the camps dies. Those are your choices—and you cannot afford to hesitate."

The electric gun vibrated in my palm, warm and ready.

Jayde grabbed my shoulders and steered me around so I was standing square in a booth. "We'll start slow and easy with a non-moving target."

How is that any easier? If anything, it made it worse. The holographic man was just standing there, taking it. Unarmed. Innocent.

Jayde stepped back. "Shoot him."

Instinctively, I put my body in position, sliding one foot back and steadying the gun with both hands. But I did not put my finger on the trigger.

"Shoot him," Jayde repeated, less kindly.

I slid my finger over the trigger and willed myself to pull it, but I couldn't. *It's just a hologram!* I derided myself. *Just do it and get it over with!*

"Phil," Jayde threatened, all of the patience leaving his voice.

I tried, I really tried to pull the trigger, but the world was frozen. I couldn't breathe. I couldn't feel my heartbeat. My fingers were cramped and stiff, like rigor mortis had set in early. All I could hear over and over was the scream of my soul, the last sliver of my identity begging for its life.

I am not a killer I am not a killer I am not a killer!

Jayde sighed loud enough for me to hear him through the earbuds. There was a beep, and suddenly, the hologram came to life. The man lurched into motion, face contorting in rage. A knife spawned in his hand. Without even a flicker of hesitation, he roared and charged at me.

I screamed and fired.

The shot shattered the air like thunder. The electric bullet arced forward and hit the man square in the chest. The hologram shattered into a million pieces, scattering on the floor like spilled rice.

I braced myself against the booth wall as the adrenaline collapsed like a demolished building. The hologram faded, but the image was burned in my memory. I played it over and over—the crack of the bullet, the gasp of the breath leaving his lungs, the roll of his eyes as his mind went dark.

You killed him.

"Good." Jayde's voice echoed from far away, bobbing in on the waves of nausea that coursed through my system. "Restart program."

The hologram regenerated in the middle of the room, a different man this time. This one was bigger, angrier. I swallowed. "How many times do I…"

"Until I'm confident you can pull the trigger."

The image flickered, and my digital assailant roused himself, wicked glare focusing on me. He shifted, then reached into his jacket and withdrew a gun.

I shot first.

"Better," Jayde grunted. "Again."

I stared at the pixels as they melted into a pool of blood on the floor. Jayde's words echoed in my head like a fading gunshot.

Until I'm confident you can pull the trigger. Until I'm confident you can kill.

12

"Again" turned into three days of solid training.

Jayde kept me in the range most of the rest of the day. We broke only to meet with Tower and a few other officers to debrief them on the operation as the morbid details came together.

Jayde would be going with me to Beijing. He had worked for Thames, which meant he technically worked for me. It was very easy to draw up a contract and claim he was my bodyguard. Even Asia fell for the ruse; when I told her Jayde would be flying with me, she didn't even bat an eyelash.

Meanwhile, Blue Fire went into hibernation. I recorded a short video claiming my position had been compromised and I needed to lay low for a few weeks. Jayde crafted my script carefully. It was worded so that Asia would believe I was stepping down; if I gave her any reason to suspect I had ulterior motives for coming to Beijing, it would all be over.

She texted me a mere thirty minutes after the video went up to say she was proud of me for making such a brave decision.

Privately, I also hoped Nic would see the video. Maybe if he thought I was taking his advice and retiring, he'd leave me alone and not ask questions.

So far, it was working. He texted once to make sure I still had the reservations for my transit flight to Mars. When I showed him the confirmation receipt, he went mercifully silent.

My followers were less accepting of my retirement. The comments on the video descended into a hailstorm of panic, fear, and accusations. Some people claimed they would quit if I wasn't involved. Jayde and his team worked tirelessly to try and convince people that Operation Blue Fire was still on, but the damage had been done.

The people would understand as soon as they saw the footage of me assassinating the General Secretary.

Tower took me home that night. He, as usual, did not have much to say. But he did tell me that he was proud of me.

I asked him if he thought Dad would be proud too. He didn't have an answer for that.

The next day was more of the same, only this time, the training was worse. Every time I shot a hologram, Jayde would load another one, not even pausing to let me process the virtual life I'd just taken. I killed again, and again, and again, but it was never enough for Jayde.

As the day wore on, I could have sworn that the projections began to look familiar. At first, I thought I was hallucinating it, my exhaustion projecting ghosts that weren't there. But, one by one, I started to recognize the digital faces.

At first, it was just people I'd heard of on the news. United officials, councilmen, military generals. But slowly the likenesses grew closer to home. The district governor, the chief of the Boston police, the principal of my old school.

Lieutenant Clint.

I failed that one. Jayde tried a dozen simulations with a dozen scenarios, and each time I hesitated a beat too long. No matter how cruel and threatening and dangerous the computer made Clint appear, all I could see was the fear in his eyes as he gave up the radio to save his life.

I begged Jayde to change the program. He refused. Again and again the computer threw the hologram of Clint at me, and again and again I spared his life at the expense of my own. No matter how much Jayde coached me, no matter how bitterly he cussed me out, I couldn't do it.

Tower finally rescued me when he came to say it was time to go home.

I passed out as soon as dinner was over, but I regretted sleeping when my dreams became a repeat of the simulation. All night long, I saw Clint lying on the sidewalk. This time, he was injured, bloody, and helpless. He groveled on the concrete and begged me to spare his life.

But in this dream, I didn't. In this dream, when Jayde told me to fire, I did.

In a cruel irony, I overslept. Mrs. Von finally came and roused me, saying I had company. I stumbled down to the kitchen to find Stanyard sitting at the counter. He'd clearly been there awhile; his plate was licked clean, and he was on his second cup of coffee.

He shoved his stool back as soon as I entered. "Phil—Andi, are you okay?"

"I'm fine," I croaked, even though everything about my appearance sent the opposite message.

He wasn't blind. "No, you're not." He strode over and opened his arms like he was about to hug me. My heart lurched at the same time my body recoiled. I wanted to collapse in his arms and sob, but I knew that was the last thing I should be doing. I couldn't tell him what was wrong. I couldn't tell him what I was training for. He couldn't know about any of this. As far as he was concerned, everything was fine.

And I knew that if he touched me, I wouldn't be able to lie to him again.

I stepped back and put my hand up. "I just couldn't sleep. I'm… sore from all the training. Please don't touch me."

He obeyed.

No sooner had I stepped foot on base than Jayde summoned me back to the range. "Jayde, please," I begged. "I can't do this today." Everything still hurt, and I had a blinding headache. Never mind the fact that I felt like I could have a mental breakdown at any moment.

"You're not leaving this room until you pass this test," he announced without even looking at me, and I knew he meant it.

I heard the door creak and turned to see Stanyard slip in. *No, anyone but him. I can't let him see this. I can't let him see me kill.*

Jayde put the visor and earbuds in my hands. "Again."

"But…" I hesitated, my eyes still on Stanyard.

"The sooner you do this, the sooner you can leave. Again." He thrust the gun at me.

I shoved the earbuds in and grabbed the weapon with a growl. Snapping the visor on, I whipped around to face the range. "Make it quick."

Stanyard's voice echoed hesitantly through the earbuds. "Phil…"

"Shut up," Jayde snapped at him. He punched the control panel, and the simulation flickered to life. There was Clint, in fatigues and carrying a rifle that was practically bigger than I was.

My anger wavered.

"Ready, set… shoot!" Jayde barked.

The simulation lurched to life. Clint charged at me, and I felt my muscles seizing up, the fear clenching my nerves.

I closed my eyes to block out the image and fired. *It's not real. It's not real!*

The program shrieked as the hologram died. I turned away, unwilling to look at the digital remains, and pushed the visor up on my forehead. "There. You happy?" I spat at Jayde.

He shook his head. "This time, eyes open."

I moaned and turned around, suddenly aware that my headache was worse. It was thicker, heavier, the weight shifting to one side of my head as if my whole body were out of balance. I braced myself against the booth wall.

"Again," Jayde shouted, and Clint reappeared. This time, all he had was a knife.

I pried my eyes open, willing myself not to blink, as I mechanically raised the gun and fired. The hologram disintegrated, and I winced. Was it just me, or were the colors getting brighter? I blinked, but ghosts of Clint's face still danced across my vision. Was the visor malfunctioning?

"Again."

The room went dark, and for a minute, I could see no one. Then I heard scuffling, and I looked down.

Clint lay on the ground a few yards away, moaning.

Oh God, no.

"Shoot him," Jayde commanded from somewhere behind me.

I can't.

"He's not innocent, Phil," Jayde coached, as if he could read my thoughts. "He's part of the system. He's the problem."

I took a step forward. Clint jerked around, his wild eyes searching mine. His hand cradled some unseen injury as he panted for breath.

"But he's injured," I argued, this time aloud. "He can't hurt me."

He never hurt me. Clint had been the warden, yes, but he had been reasonable. He'd never been cruel. He'd never touched me, never threatened me, never demanded more than what was expected of him. He'd never been a threat to me.

"Doesn't matter," Jayde spat. "Even if he's just pushing paperwork, he's helping the enemy."

I took another step forward, then another, feeling the floor of the range slope upwards beneath my feet.

"The government and anyone who helps them is the enemy, Phil." Jayde's voice came through loud and clear, louder than the throbbing in my ears. "If you don't stop them, they'll kill everyone you love. Do you want to be responsible for that?"

I flinched, the accusations of a thousand failures washing over me. No, I didn't want to be responsible for the loss of any more life. I couldn't. I had to save them.

I stopped only a few inches away from Clint. I put my foot back and lifted the weapon.

"Remember who the enemy is, Phil."

I am Blue Fire.

"Kill him."

And this is my war.

I fired.

The hologram shattered with a scream—a scream that kept echoing and echoing. My ears started ringing as the sound continued to ricochet, as if the explosion from the gun never stopped. My headache throbbed, and random colors flashed across the room. Was the hologram glitching? Where was Jayde? What was happening?

I took a step back, but the floor wasn't there. My mind pitched like a ship rolled by a wave as I fell.

"Phil!" Stanyard screeched, and caught me as the world went black.

13

"I'm not going to ask what you were doing. I'm just going to tell you that you were doing it wrong."

I'd only blacked out for a second. I came to as Stanyard was carrying me to the elevator. I heard Jayde in the background, radioing for Mrs. Nolan. I tried to tell Stanyard that I could stand on my own, but he ignored me. He didn't even look me in the eye. I just felt his arms tighten around me as the elevator rushed upwards.

I almost had my bearings back by the time we arrived in the lab, but Mrs. Nolan promptly stabbed me with a needle, and I lost them again. Everything suddenly became warm and fuzzy and *oh so calm*. I didn't resist as Stanyard laid me in a chair and Mrs. Nolan threaded an IV into my arm. I just sat there, completely unaware of the passage of time, watching the fluid *drip, drip, drip* down the tube.

I might have slept. I wasn't sure. It was the middle of the afternoon by the time I finally got a grip on my surroundings. I sat up and stretched, slowly, finally regaining control of my muscles.

I looked around the room. Stanyard was gone. Mrs. Nolan stood over Dad's incubator, typing notes into a tablet. She heard me moving and started lecturing without even looking up.

"If you're going to traumatize yourself, at least try to stay hydrated."

"Sorry," I mumbled.

"You're fine," she answered my unspoken question. She set her tablet down and came over to remove the IV. "But you need to rest. And yes, I already told Jayde."

I held still while she pulled the needle from my arm, then stood up and tested my balance. Mercifully, the world stayed upright.

Mrs. Nolan walked back to Dad's machine. "When are you leaving for Beijing?"

I froze. "How did you—"

"Jayde told me." She adjusted a dial on the control pad. "Asked me if I would go with you."

A shot of hope ramrodded my heart. "Will you?"

She shook her head and picked up the tablet. "You don't need me."

"Yes, I do," I insisted. "You've been there. You know these people. You know how to dress, how to act…"

She snorted. "Don't worry, Asia will tell you everything you need to know. I'm sure she has it all planned out already."

"But…" I struggled to quantify why her disinterest was so disappointing. "I thought this is what you wanted."

"It was," she admitted, too quickly. "But you're not going to Beijing because you want to be a Nolan, are you?" She glanced back at me then, one eyebrow raised in accusation.

I swallowed. "How much did Jayde tell you?"

"Not much." She resumed typing notes into the tablet with one hand. "But I know you better than you think. And I know this is not what you want."

Which part? I almost blurted, but caught myself.

"I just hope you realize what you're throwing away."

I stiffened. "What?"

She kept her back to me, swiping aimlessly on the tablet. "We gave you a gift. Andromeda was a gift, and she's irreplaceable."

The clump of anxiety found its way to my throat again when I realized she was right. As soon as I shook the General's hand, Andromeda's spotless reputation would be ruined. I'd no longer be able to hide behind my clean file, my money, and my privilege.

"It's your choice what to do with her," Mrs. Nolan continued, the permission in her voice a blank check. "It always was. Just know that once Andromeda is dead, even Asia won't be able to bring her back to life."

It was true. By midnight Saturday, Andromeda would be dead—just like Philadelphia was. Would Philadelphia get to come back to life from the ashes? Or would I just be Blue Fire?

Did it matter? Did it matter who I was if I could save my friends, my family? Wasn't that why I had been given these identities—so I could make a difference?

"Do you want me to keep him under until you get back?"

I started as Mrs. Nolan's words splashed me in the face with a consequence I hadn't even considered. *My father.* We were supposed to be waking my father up tomorrow. And I wouldn't be here for him; I'd already be on the flight to China.

I walked over and stared down at my father's sleeping face. He was beginning to look more like a living person; his skin had developed some color, and he was regaining weight. He was almost completely weaned off life support, and only a few wires were still connected to his wrist and his head. His chest rose and fell gently as he breathed on his own, the inside of the oxygen mask fogging with each exhale.

"Can you do that?" I asked, looking across the machine at Mrs. Nolan.

She shrugged. "He's been under this long. Another week won't hurt him."

I almost said yes. I wanted to be selfish, to keep my father under until I was ready to deal with the tragedy of his new existence on my own terms. But that wasn't fair to him. My dad deserved a chance at life, whatever that life might look like.

I slipped my hand into the incubator and grasped Dad's limp fingers. "No. Do what you need to do. I trust you," I declared, and I meant it.

Tower took me home shortly after, where I discovered that coming home early was just as traumatic for the Vons as getting home late. Fortunately, Mr. Von was easily appeased when I agreed to watch TV with him for the rest of the day. After all, I was under doctor's orders to do nothing, and watching mindless sitcoms was the most effective way to keep my complicated thoughts offline.

We'd finished dinner and started on a new show when I became aware of an incessant ringing. It was faint and distant, and I thought it was coming from the TV at first. But when it wouldn't stop—and neither Mr. nor Mrs. Von made any move to answer it—I got up.

I excused myself and walked out into the hall. I could hear it more clearly now; it was coming from upstairs, from Cea's bedroom.

And that's when I recognized the ringtone. It was my tablet.

I charged up the stairs and threw the bedroom door open. My tablet almost vibrated off the nightstand as it rang again and again. It rang out as soon as I picked up the device. The home screen was cluttered with notifications for ten missed calls.

Before I could unlock it and read the caller ID, the device rang again.

Nic.

I almost didn't answer. I didn't want to talk to him, but worry outweighed my reserve. Nic never called me. Told me to call him, yes. Called other people and demanded to know where I was, also yes. But he'd never once initiated a call with me, and if he'd called ten times in a row, it must be bad news.

What if something's wrong with Ephesus's transit? That was the worst but most plausible explanation I could think of. I offered up a quick prayer and answered the call. "What's wrong?"

"Why don't you tell me?"

His voice came through before the video did, but I didn't need a camera to tell me what expression he was wearing. He was angry. Very, very angry.

"N-nothing's wrong," I stuttered. "You're the one that called me."

"And why do you think that is?" His video connected, bringing me face to face with his fury. He was using a handheld device, and he leered creepily close to the camera, his head filling the entire screen.

I held my tablet away from me, as if that could restore my personal space. "I-I don't know!" I yelled, and my confusion was genuine. As far as he knew, there was nothing wrong. Unless…

He confirmed my worst fears when he spat, "You're not planning on coming back to Mars, are you?"

I was too stunned to answer, and that was all the confirmation he needed. His face contorted with rage—and then, suddenly, he relaxed. He blinked, as if he'd just woken up out of a dead sleep and was adjusting to reality.

When he finally spoke, his voice was calm, a statement. "You lied to me."

"I didn't lie," I snapped, faster than I could recognize that I'd just done it again.

"No, I suppose not," he grunted, the sarcasm returning like a layer of smoke. "You just conveniently changed your mind after booking the transit tickets."

Unironically, he wasn't wrong. But that was because so much had changed—so much he didn't know about. "Nic, they're closing the camps. They're going to deport everyone to—"

"I have eyes. I saw the news. What I want to know is what you're planning on doing about it, and why it involves you shooting men in the face until you pass out."

My retort died on my tongue. "How did you—"

"Stanyard told me."

I sank down on the bed as this information altered the playing field.

Nic did the same, sitting in a chair and holding the camera a safe distance away from his face. "Phil," he sighed, the concern overriding the bitterness in his voice. "What's going on?"

I wished he would stay angry. It was so much easier to refuse him when he was angry.

"I—I can't tell you," I managed, and braced myself.

He worked his jaw in silence for a minute before replying. "What's scary is that I actually believe that."

I stared down at the screen.

He shifted so he was square in the frame. "Are you being threatened?"

I shook my head rapidly. "No, no—it's just classified."

"Always is. Are you in danger?"

Not immediately. I shook my head again. "I'm fine. I just overdid it today, I promise."

"Okay, then you can tell me what's going on."

It was not a suggestion. "But, Nic, I—"

"Phil," he interrupted, but not unkindly, "whatever it is, I promise I can protect you. And I promise that no one will know we had this conversation. You can talk to me."

I grasped at the only other excuse I could think of. "I don't want to put you in danger—"

"Hasn't stopped you yet."

It was spoken dryly, but that was all it took to release the dam of memories.

Look, I'm aware Andromeda has put herself—and, quite frankly, the rest of us—in a dangerous position. But that was her choice.

"Phil," Nic said, speaking in time with the images flashing through my mind.

It's a risk I'm willing to take. Start talking.

"Talk to me."

The door's still open.

"I can't help you if you don't tell me what's going on."

I dragged my knuckles across my face, pushing the emotion back in. "I'm going to China."

If that revelation surprised him, he covered it well. "When?"

"Tomorrow."

"Why?"

I closed my eyes and tried to find the same conviction I'd had yesterday. "I was invited to the state dinner—"

He swore.

There was a beat, and then he did it again. And again. He threw his device down and stormed out of frame, repeating the same swear word over and over.

"Nic—"

"Why are you going?" he snapped from off-camera.

I couldn't decipher his tone of voice, and that made me panic. "I—I'm going to meet the General Secretary," I stammered.

Silence.

"And I'm going to shake his hand."

Still more silence.

"And I… I'm going to kill him."

The confession sucked the breath from my lungs in a gasp. Jayde had talked about it, we'd been planning it, and I'd been training for it. But I'd never actually said it, admitted it.

I am going to kill the General Secretary.

"You're lying," Nic declared, voice cool.

"What? No! That's the truth, Nic, I swear." I shook the tablet, as if that could force him back into frame. I expected him to be upset. I didn't expect him to not believe me at all.

He answered the summons, reappearing and picking up his device. "Then you're lying about being threatened. Who's in charge? Is it that carrot-topped military brat?"

"Jayde? Yes—I mean, no, I mean, I'm doing this willingly. We're in this together."

"Then you're both idiots." He delivered the insult effortlessly, like a backhanded slap. "You can't kill. Who do you think you are, Phil?"

I am Blue Fire. "Yes, I can, and I will."

His entire face puckered as he snorted. "Really? What are you going to do? Throw the Bible at him?"

I'm about to throw the Bible at you. "Of course not. I'm going to shake his hand."

Nic contorted his eyebrows and looked downright amused, like I'd just said I was going to sprinkle pixie dust on the General and turn him into a frog.

I glared at him. "You don't believe me, do you?"

"Oh, I believe you," he chirped. "I'm just waiting for you to realize how *incredibly* stupid and childish you're being right now. What did I tell you about being a hero?"

I stiffened. "There's a computer embedded in my palm. It's programmed to his DNA. As soon as I shake his hand, he'll have a heart attack." I thrust my hand at the camera. "Call Andes if you don't believe me. He installed it."

He blinked at the screen, nursing the silence for a long moment. "You're serious."

"I have been this entire time."

He sighed, a long, grating sound that caused the connection to crackle. "You're coming home."

Not this again. "No, I'm not. Are you even listening to me?"

"Regrettably, I am, and I'm done bargaining with you." His fingers swiped across the screen as he toggled menus in the background. "Pack your bags. I'm calling the police. They'll put you on the next transit."

My cheeks burned, but I held my ground. "I'm not going."

"Tell that to CPS."

I volleyed the threat right back at him. "They can take it up with Jayde."

He stopped, wisely deduced that physical threats wouldn't work, and resumed the verbal abuse. "You're a fool."

My cheeks burned as his words fed the monster of shame that lurked just below my heart. But I steeled my nerves and pushed past the feeling. I would not let him bully me, not this time. "No, I'm not."

"You're right, my bad. You're a hypocrite, which is even worse."

My self-control shattered beneath the accusation. I'd been called a lot of things by a lot of people, but hypocrite was never one of them. "Excuse me?"

"I mean, if I knew you wanted to play dirty, we could have saved ourselves a lot of trouble and just finished Red Rain."

It was spoken frivolously, heartlessly—and with so much hate.

Every nerve in my spine bristled with the implication. "This isn't like that! I'm not like you."

"A shame, really. At least my plan for WWIV had *style*."

Did he honestly think that was what I was trying to do? Did he honestly think I intended to slaughter *millions* of people just to get my way? "I'm not trying to start a war—I'm trying to end one."

He squinted one eye shut. "By murdering the highest government official on live TV at a party surrounded by his most loyal followers? That's not how politics *or* parties work."

"No, don't you see?" I begged, even though it was clear to both of us that he didn't. "I can get close to him. I can do this cleanly. This is why I'm a Nolan. This is why I'm here. God chose me!"

He laughed, the abrupt sound causing his video to glitch. "God didn't 'choose' you for anything, Phil. You're delusional."

"And you're a coward."

The accusation left my mouth before I had time to filter it. It hung there, echoing in the sudden silence between us.

That was when I finally admitted how true those words were—and how long I had wanted to say them.

"You have no idea what it's like to be unassimilated," I continued, my feelings slowly forming a usable shape out of the darkness. "You have no idea what it's like to live in a camp and be told you're worthless because of your faith. You've always had privilege, and money, and your college degrees. All you've ever wanted was to cut yourself off from the world and live in your own little kingdom, safe and protected from everyone's problems."

He didn't deny it. He just stared at the screen, his face stoic, unyielding.

"Well, I'm sorry, but my world doesn't work like that. For the first time in my life, I have power, and I'm going to do something with it. I'm not going to run back to Mars and hide while the world burns. I'm not like you."

As I spoke, I began to see the chasm between us for what it really was.

He saw it too. "Is that what you think of me?" It was a statement, not a question.

It was too late to lie, so I told him the truth. "I think you only care about yourself. That's why you created Red Rain. You don't care about Earth or the unassimilated. You don't care about freedom. You don't care about Ephesus, or Cea, or my dad. You don't care about me."

And you never did.

He finally moved, shifting and sitting up straight. His voice was calm and cold, the same tone he'd used when we first met on Mars.

"I'm disappointed in you, Philadelphia."

Then his screen flickered and went blank.

Did he hang up on me? I tapped his avatar and got a horrendous screech in reply. An error message popped up, and I stared at the contents in disbelief.

He'd blocked me.

14

"Resume program."

The gun range was mercifully empty when I arrived on base the next day. I'd called and asked Tower to pick me up in the morning, because he was the only one I could trust not to ask questions. Stanyard was nowhere to be found when we entered the lobby, and neither was Jayde. He'd texted to say he was making the final preparations to install the microchip in my palm—the piece of programming that would turn the computer in my hand from an inert web of wires into a targeted weapon.

I would be meeting him in the lab in an hour. After that, we would go by the Vons to pick up my tablet and luggage and say goodbye, not that I expected them to remember I was leaving. Then we would meet Asia at the airport, and I'd be on my way to Beijing.

That meant I had an hour to kill. And kill was exactly what I wanted to do.

The visor and gun were abandoned on the floor in the middle of the range, right where I'd dropped them yesterday. The simulation was still loaded on the control panel. Donning a pair of earbuds, I retrieved the gun and visor and centered myself in a booth.

"Random opponent."

The laser light congregated in the middle of the room. Snapping the visor on, I saw that the computer had generated some nameless military officer. *Perfect.*

"Begin," I announced to the empty room, sliding my foot back and putting the gun in position.

The hologram roused himself. I waited until he had taken two steps and then shot him where he stood.

"Again."

The computer continued to spawn random assailants. Most of them were faceless, but a few I recognized. It didn't matter. I took them all down, most of them before they even had time to draw their weapon.

I let the next one get closer. He charged at me with a knife, mouth open in a primal scream. He was a mere two feet from me—so close that I could see the glitching in his soulless eyes—before I dropped him.

I watched his pixels disintegrate and sighed. This was too easy.

"Increase difficulty level by twenty-five percent."

The computer rose to the challenge. It began to spawn enemies from different corners of the room; one even sprung out from the booth next to me. Some of them hit the ground running; many of them had their weapons already drawn. I missed several of them, but it didn't matter. Anything for a challenge. Anything to feel something.

"See, Nic?" I hissed as I hit another square in the chest. I watched his digital remains spill at my feet. "I can do this."

The next opponent generated in the corner next to the booths. I lunged out from around the metal divider and shot him—but not before he got a shot in at me. The digital bullet arced past my shoulder, barely missing me, and slammed into the wall with a shower of sparks.

I stared at the pixels as they faded away, relishing the adrenaline that pounded in my chest. Beneath the panic of near-death, I felt a new sensation, one I'd never felt before. Victory. Power. Pride.

I am one of them.

Jayde had been right about me all along. This was where I belonged. I didn't belong in a camp. I didn't belong on Mars. And I definitely didn't belong in Washington or Beijing with the elites. This—this is who I was.

"No, it's not."

I whipped around. The voice came from the next opponent: Lieutenant Clint.

He strolled towards me from the far side of the room. He was unarmed, but I shot him anyway.

He respawned in the opposite corner. "You won't shoot me."

I proved him wrong. He immediately reappeared.

"Random opponent!" I yelled at the computer, but nothing happened. *What is wrong with this thing?*

Clint continued to approach slowly, as if he'd cleared his afternoon and had nowhere better to be. "I know you, Philadelphia."

"You don't know me!" I shouted, but my voice came back warbly and distant through the earplugs. He couldn't hear me—nobody could hear me.

I shot him again, and he respawned mid-laugh. "Look at you. This is pathetic."

He stopped in the middle of the floor and waited until I took him out for the fourth time. He reappeared in exactly the same spot, his head wagging in a derisive gesture I knew all too well. "Isn't it about time you came home?"

"I am home!" I screeched, and fired.

His hologram didn't even disintegrate this time. He just stared at the hole I'd made in his virtual chest and snorted. The image flickered, and he regenerated, good as new. "You're not a hero, Andromeda."

I killed him almost before he got the words out. "Yes, I am!"

The image blinked and respawned, so I shot him again.

"You can't control me!"

And again.

"You don't get to decide who I am!"

And again. The explosions echoed around the room, layering one on top of the other in a broken symphony. The hologram pulsed as it respawned over and over.

I strode up to him. He didn't move, just sneered down his nose at me as if I were no more annoying than a stray cat.

I shoved the gun under his chin, savoring the rush of power as the hologram glitched and struggled to recalibrate.

I stood on my toes until my eyes were mere inches from his. "And I don't need you."

"Phil!"

I whipped around. The computer had spawned a second opponent, and he was running right at me, his entire frame glowing red.

I took aim.

"Wait! Don't shoot!" He skidded to a stop.

"I will!" I threatened. "Don't come any closer!"

He raised his hands in surrender. "Phil, it's me!"

The familiar voice cut through my subconscious, and that's when I remembered that holograms weren't red. Red meant it was a real person.

I yanked the visor off. *Stanyard.*

He stood a few yards away, panting, his eyes wild with fear as he looked between me and the gun.

The weapon clattered to the floor.

He lowered his hands. "What are you doing?"

I spun around, but Clint was gone. In fact, the whole program was off, the range dark. Dozens of scorch marks peppered the walls and floor where I had shot at a hundred imaginary opponents.

I buckled and landed on my knees, hard.

Stanyard kicked the gun a safe distance away and dropped down beside me. "Phil, you're sweating. What's wrong?"

I swiped a hand across my forehead and stared at the perspiration glistening on my fingertips—the fingertips that had almost pulled the trigger on my best friend.

"I almost killed you," I whispered.

He said nothing.

"I almost killed you!" I repeated, louder. I looked up at him and begged him to corroborate the story. I had no idea what was real anymore.

"Yes," he said, very slowly. "You did."

I wanted to apologize, but the words clogged in my throat. *What have you become?*

"Phil…" Stanyard grabbed my hand, and his touch ignited a dozen emotions I wasn't prepared to feel—didn't *deserve* to feel. Stanyard deserved better. He deserved someone who didn't scream at him, hit him, try to kill him. He deserved someone who didn't lie to him.

My dad had lied to my mom. He'd lied and failed to involve her in his revolution, and that's why she died. And now I was doing the exact same thing to the friend who had tried so many times to save me.

I tried to yank my arm from his grasp and stand up. "I need to go."

"No, Phil, please!" He tightened his grip and pulled me back down to the ground. "Don't do this to me. Don't shut me out."

"But I—"

"I can't lose you again."

I stopped and stared at him as memories of his panicked text messages came rushing back.

I THOUGHT I LOST YOU

He took a breath and shifted, sitting cross-legged next to me. "Do you know what the worst moment of my life was?"

"When you left camp?"

He snorted. "No."

"When you… left me in the alley?" That wasn't necessarily the worst moment of my life either, but it was definitely on the list.

He shook his head. "No. It was when you blocked me, after you asked me to check if the road was clear."

I remembered. I hadn't known it was Stanyard then; I'd known him only by his online alias, Aurelius, and I thought it was Jayde talking. I was being chased by cops and had asked him to radio and see if the intersection was clear. The underground had used the opportunity to catch up to me.

That's when I realized I'd been lied to and cut Aurelius off.

"As soon as you hung up on me, I realized something bad was about to happen—and it would be my fault because I was too afraid to tell you the truth. If I had just told you who I was and apologized in the first place, none of that—Carnegie, your dad getting frozen—would have ever happened."

I searched his face and tried to imagine that alternate universe. I didn't blame him at all—I'd made a lot of mistakes and brought most of my misery on myself—but he wasn't wrong. If I had known it was him, things would have gone very differently.

Stanyard cradled my hand in both of his, rubbing my knuckles with his thumbs. "I made the same mistake with Mira. She started changing, going down a path I knew was wrong, and I didn't say anything. I stayed quiet and played the supportive older brother because I didn't want her to shut me out."

I thought of Mira's dramatic change in appearance and suddenly realized why Stanyard had been so upset about my tattoo. It wasn't about the ink; it was because he'd seen this all before and knew how it ended.

He stared at my shoulder. "Can I see?"

I loosened my hand from his and rolled my sleeve up, revealing the emblem permanently etched on my upper arm: a thunderbird.

I tried to read his reaction, but there was no emotion on his face. "Do you like it?" I ventured.

His eyes returned to mine. "Do you want the truth?"

"Yes," I said, even though my heart said no.

"I'm not a big fan of tattoos," he admitted, "but what concerns me is what it means."

I jumped to the inevitable conclusion. "You don't think I should do this."

"Phil, I don't even know what 'this' is anymore. I…" He took a deep breath, closed his eyes, and tried again. "Look, after what happened with your dad, I promised myself—and God—that if I was ever worried about one of my friends again, I'd say something. I would tell them the truth, no matter how it made me feel. No matter if they rejected me."

Heat flashed across my cheeks.

He opened his eyes and bravely met my stare. "I'm going to tell you how I feel. And when I'm done, if you want to tell me it's none of my business, then okay. But please, just hear me out."

I nodded.

He found my hands again. "I'm worried about you. I know you and Jayde are planning something, and the fact that it involves you training to kill concerns me. You've been withdrawn and anxious, and you're avoiding everyone. That's why I called Nic."

I winced and looked down at my lap. Stanyard was right; I'd been pushing away everyone who was trying to help me. Especially Nic.

Stanyard squeezed my hands. "Did you talk to him?"

I nodded, and the motion shook loose the grief I'd been avoiding since last night. I'd ruined my friendship with Nic, and now I couldn't even get a hold of him to apologize if I wanted to.

A few tears fell and splattered on Stanyard's hand.

He pulled me closer, and I let him. I laid my head on his shoulder and tried to find the words, the emotions, the prayers I needed to express what I had to say.

He wrapped his arms around me and spoke gently in my ear. "Can you tell me?"

Underneath the chaos in my soul, I felt the tiniest whisper of the Holy Spirit. *You can talk to him.*

"I'll—I'll try," I said, and obeyed. In between sobs and bursts of silence as I tried to come to grips with what had happened, I told Stanyard everything. About Operation Thunderbird, about the implant in my palm, about my argument with Nic.

I broke down crying then. Stanyard just held me, praying in tongues under his breath, and waited until my tears had dried.

He set me upright and brushed my tangled hair out of my face. "What do you think you should do?"

I stalled my answer by rubbing my eyes with my palms. "I... I don't know."

"Why not? What's holding you back?" he said in a way that suggested he'd already come up with his own answer.

I wished it was that easy for me. "I just... I just don't see how this *can't* be God. Me being Blue Fire..." I traced my hands in the air like I was connecting strings on a corkboard. "Too much has happened for this to *not* be God. This can't be a mistake. I can't be making this up."

"I agree," he said with conviction.

A small bit of reassurance found its way into my heart, so I pressed on. "And this party... I mean, it's on my *birthday*. How is that an accident?"

"It's not."

"So why..." I looked up at the scorch-marked ceiling and tried to order my thoughts like a deck of cards. "So why am I here, if not for this? I didn't choose this. Thames chose *me*, and Asia has gone out of her way to make me a Nolan. God clearly gave me this identity for a reason. If not this, then why?"

"I don't know," Stanyard admitted. He tapped his finger on the concrete, giving us both a minute to think. "But you've never stopped to find out."

I frowned at him.

He shrugged and spread his hands. "I think you're right. I think God made you a Nolan for a reason. But I think you've spent the last two months running from Andromeda instead of asking why she exists."

He was right again. I'd only adopted the identity to survive. Up until a few days ago, I'd never intended to be a Nolan in anything more than name. I never saw Thames as anything more than an enemy, and Mrs. Nolan was only an unfortunate ally. I'd never once asked God why all this had happened to me.

"Did you ask Him about the mission, Phil?"

I blinked and focused on Stanyard's face.

"Did you ask Him if He wants you to kill the General?"

I didn't say anything. The burn on my cheeks was answer enough. I hadn't prayed about this—I hadn't prayed about this at all. I'd just assumed, because there had been so much happenstance and coincidence and miracle involved in getting me there, that it must be God. I hadn't actually asked Him what He wanted me to do.

Because, I realized just then, I'd been afraid of the answer.

"What do you think He'll say?" Stanyard prodded.

I closed my eyes and turned my thoughts inward. The answer was instantaneous, like it had been hovering in my peripheral the whole time. I just had to turn and look.

I opened my eyes. "I need to talk to Jayde."

Stanyard scrambled up and offered his hand. "Do you want me to come with you?"

I let him help me to my feet. "No, this is something I have to do."

His phone buzzed. He pulled it out of his pocket and glanced at the screen. "Looks like I have to go back to work anyway. Come find me afterwards?" He followed me to the door.

"Of course. And hey." I turned and touched his elbow. I waited until he met my eyes, then forced as much overdue gratitude into my words as I could. "Thank you."

His face warmed in a smile that sparkled deep behind his eyes. "I'd do anything for you."

He would, and he had.

"If it means anything…" He gently grasped my shoulders. "I think you're making the right decision."

"That means everything," I said, and it was the truth.

"Killing… that's not you." His thumb pinched my shoulder where my tattoo was. "You don't kill people, Phil. You save them. You give them second chances when they don't deserve them—like me."

My heart flinched. "Of course you deserved a second chance. Everyone does."

He chuckled. "And there she is. *That's* the Philadelphia I know."

I sucked in my breath. Stanyard rarely used my full name, but I liked the way he said it: slow and sweet, like he had all the time in the world for me.

"That—that compassion, that innocence—is why I believe in you. That's why I came back for you. That's why I…"

He hesitated, and I felt the tension stretch out between us—all the unspoken gestures and emotions strung together in a line, a line that had turned us from strangers into something else.

"Why, Stanyard?" I demanded. "Why what?"

His hand brushed the hair off my neck and then stayed there. He met my eyes and declared without a flicker of doubt, "That's why I love you."

I expected my world to bottom out, but it didn't. Instead, I felt like the earth came together under my feet, like I had something to stand on, rely on. Someone who would support me no matter what, someone whose arms would catch me if I fell. Someone who loved me for who I was. Not for what I could do. Not for any of the titles I wore. But for me.

I wanted to tell him all of that, but words seemed cheap. So I kissed him instead.

He reciprocated—gently, sweetly, one hand cradling the back of my head. The kiss was short—too short—but he held me for a moment longer, letting our silence put a period on the promise we'd just exchanged.

When he finally pulled away, he was grinning. "I'll take that as a yes."

"Yes," I laughed, "I love you too."

15

The flutter in my stomach lasted to the elevator, and that's where the giddy feeling ended.

I braced myself against the wall as I ascended alone, forcing my breaths to be slow and steady. My heart continued to pulse, this time for an entirely different reason. I knew how this conversation would go, and it would not be pleasant.

Holy Spirit, I need you now.

Jayde was waiting for me in a lab on the tenth floor. He stood behind a worktable with a young man I didn't recognize. They were both bent over a laptop that looked advanced enough to be sentient. Scattered on the table was a morbid array of implements and wires.

In the center of it all was the kill chip.

It was microscopic; it would have fit on the eraser of a pencil. It was plugged into a docking port and shielded by a glass case. The port's flashing lights illuminated the miniature circuitry as it sat there, taunting me with the morbid reality of what I'd almost done, what I'd almost become.

The men stopped their conversation as soon as I entered. Jayde didn't greet me, but the other man offered me a cavernous smile. "Blue Fire!"

I deferred with a nod.

He slammed the laptop shut and unplugged it from the docking port. "You're good to go, man."

Jayde clasped his arm in a brawny handshake. "Send the bill."

"You know it." The man came around the table and gripped my hand in both of his. "It's an honor to finally meet you. Data."

I remembered hearing the callsign on the radio back when I was trying to make contact with my father. "Charmed," I responded.

"Good luck," he said, and pumped my hand one more time. Then he threw a salute at Jayde and let himself out.

Jayde was fiddling with a device and didn't look up at me. "Shut the door."

I obeyed, leaning against it and taking a long breath through my nose.

Jayde arched an eyebrow. "Everything good?"

I pushed away from the door. "Yes," I said, because in a way, it was. I walked over to the table. "Jayde, we need to talk."

"Do we?" He flicked the device on. It was shaped like a gun, but I could see the tip held a laser-guided needle, not unlike the machine Andes used to alter fingerprints.

I swallowed when I realized what it was. That was the device that would implant the kill chip in my palm.

I forced the words out, drawing on the reservoir of courage the conversation with Stanyard had given me. "Yes. Jayde, I… I'm not going to do it. I'm not going to kill the General."

He slammed his hand down on the metal table with a violent smack.

I flinched but pressed on. "I'm not going to Beijing. This isn't right—this is not how we win this war."

Shadows hid his expression as he bent over the table, but I could see the tension rippling up his muscular arms. "And what," he hissed, each word like the stab of a knife, "do you suggest as an alternative?"

"I don't know," I admitted, and hated how pathetic that sounded.

"Because the only other option I see is war." He straightened, finally bringing his blackened eyes to meet mine. "Is that what you want? Would you like me to send a hundred thousand men to storm Beijing and die trying to get to the General?"

"No, but there has to be another way—"

"There is no other way!" He roared and paced in a tight circle. "Phil, there is no other way to end the United. They're too big, too powerful, and control too many resources. Either we take them down from the top, or they wipe us out. Those are the only choices."

There was always another choice. I'd proven that time and again—with Thames, with Carnegie, with Nic. There was always a third option if you were brave enough to take it. "Jayde, just listen. I—"

"No, you listen!" He whipped back around to face me. "I am sick and tired of dealing with your self-righteous idealism. The world is not a fairytale. This is life and death, and either we fight back, or they kill us all. I thought you of all people would understand that."

"Of course I understand! How do you think I got here? The only reason you even know I exist is because I wouldn't lie down and take it."

He couldn't argue with that, and his hesitation gave me enough time to get a word in edgewise. "Jayde, I'm not saying we shouldn't fight back. I'm asking you to reconsider how—"

"No, *this* is how," he cut me off, louder than before. His words escalated as he pounded the table with his fist. "We have to break the system. We have to hit them where they're weak and take out their power structure so they can't retaliate. We have to kill—"

"Maybe you're right!" I shouted.

He silenced, although whether because of my volume or my consent, I'll never know.

I took a deep breath. It did nothing to smooth my words as they tumbled over each other. "Maybe we do need war. Maybe we do need to kill the General. Maybe—maybe we should have used Red Rain. Maybe Nic was right. Maybe Thames was right."

Jayde cocked his head. "You don't believe that."

"No," I said, and with that one word, my conviction fell into place. "But I don't have to decide what's right for the world. I just have to do what's right for me."

"This isn't about you, Phil," he snapped, patience taut and fragile.

"When it's between me and God, it is." I straightened and found, for the first time in weeks, that feeling of courage beneath my feet. "I don't have the answers, and I don't need them. I don't need to decide what's right for everyone else. But I have to do what's right for *me*, what God told *me* to do. Me. Not you. Not Nic. Not even Dad."

I looked down at my right hand, pinching the motherboard beneath my skin. Jayde, Nic, Ephesus, Thames, Carnegie, even Dad—they had all made different choices, and if they were standing in my place right now, they'd probably make a different choice than I was. But I wasn't responsible for their choices. I was only responsible for mine.

I didn't know what was going to happen, but I knew one thing: God did not tell me to kill the General Secretary. This was not why I was a Nolan. This was not my time.

I looked back up at Jayde, parsing the words slowly and clearly to make sure I was understood. "I am not going to Beijing. I will be your Blue Fire. I will stay on Earth and lead this revolution. But I will not kill the General Secretary."

I braced myself for the rage, the arguments, but they never came. He just stared at me, his whole body rigid, his eyes flickering with emotions I dared not decode.

Then he shifted and pulled his phone from his pocket. He dialed and held the device out, the call on speaker for both of us to hear.

It rang once, twice, and then a distinct Russian voice picked up. "Yes, boss?"

Lev.

"Where's Stanyard?" Jayde asked, the question smooth, his eyes locked with mine.

All the air in my lungs went to my throat.

"He's here with me," Lev answered with a trace of boredom. "We're installing the new server, just like you asked."

My reality began to crack, the room shattering around the edges, as the truth caught up with me. Jayde had planned this, he'd planned it all along. He knew I might refuse and had prepared insurance.

"Do you have your gun on you?" Jayde said into the phone.

"Don't—" I started, but he put a finger to his lips.

Oh God, oh God, help.

"Always," Lev grunted. "Why?"

"If I give the signal, take Stanyard out."

Jayde spoke the command with no mercy, no fear, no regret. He arched an eyebrow and angled the phone towards me, daring me to make a sound and pull the trigger.

I said nothing.

There was rustling on the line. "Sir?" Lev repeated, and for a flicker of a moment, I could hear the scared youth in his voice. I briefly dared to hope that his innocence might be my saving grace. After all, he had been the victim of so much cruelty; surely, he wouldn't want to be the cause of more.

Jayde had no doubts. "If I give the signal, kill him," he repeated.

There was a beat, two. "Yes, boss," Lev answered finally, his voice cold again.

Jayde ended the call.

I stumbled back and gripped an exam table with both hands, digging the sharp metal edge into my fingers. "You're a monster," I hissed, but the shot felt weak, like an arrow falling short.

He shrugged and picked up the implant device. "Shall we?"

I didn't move. I stood there, frozen, scraping my mind for any excuse, any argument, any threat I could wedge into his hardened soul.

"But what about Mira?" I gasped. "You wouldn't do that to her."

He laughed, the sound hard and dry. "It was her idea."

My vision flashed red, then black.

"She won't miss him. But you will." Jayde tipped his head back and studied me. He didn't smile, but his words stretched, thin and sinister. "Don't think I haven't noticed. I've got security cameras in the range. I saw that kiss."

I tasted bile and slapped my hand over my mouth. I should have known he'd be watching, should have known he'd see what was going on between Stanyard and me. I should have been more careful.

"It's basic math, Phil." He turned to the table and scanned the contents, his fingertips grazing the array of lethal instruments. "I can sacrifice one life to save millions."

"Please," I whispered, throwing my last plea at his feet. I wanted to scream *You can't, you wouldn't*, but I knew they were lies. He could, and he would.

He selected tweezers. With a slow hand, he lifted the glass cover and removed the chip from the dock. He held it up to the harsh fluorescents like a sacrifice. "I thought you of all people would understand that equation."

I did. This was exactly why my dad had created Red Rain, why he'd bargained with the devil and given the government the keys to the apocalypse: because they'd threatened to kill me.

"My life isn't worth millions of others."

"It is to me."

A sob pushed past the blockage in my throat. I'd tried so hard for so long to undo the damage my dad had done. I'd sacrificed everything to avoid being like him, and only now did I finally understand how he felt.

And in that moment, I knew that I would be no better.

"The choice is yours." Jayde slid the chip in the chamber of the implant device and clicked it shut. "You can help me end the United, or you can die on your self-righteous hill and take Stanyard with you."

He turned to face me and held out his hand, the device throbbing and buzzing. "But I have a war to win, so I'll ask you one last time: Are you with me, Blue Fire?"

16

"You're going to love Beijing."

The inside of Asia's private jet was the most luxurious thing I'd ever seen. The interior design had been perfectly sculpted to match the plane's curves; the paneling seemed to flow off the walls, as if the whole room were in motion. The cabin was decorated in shades of white and cool gray, contrasted against real mahogany tables. Everything was rimmed with soft fluorescent lights, making it look more futuristic than the actual space stations I'd been on.

Unfortunately for me, the plane was little more than an opulent prison.

Asia sashayed up to my seat, her stiletto heels sinking into the plush carpet. "Your family has a summer home that's the envy of the neighborhood. Wait until you see the pool—do you like to swim?"

I couldn't remember the last time I'd had access to a pool, much less the desire to jump in one. "I didn't pack my swimsuit," I deferred.

Truth was, I hadn't packed *anything*. As soon as Jayde had finished implanting the device in my palm, he'd taken me down a back elevator and forced me into his car, where we'd driven straight to the transit hub. I hadn't even been allowed to say goodbye.

Asia flicked her fingers, as if the thought were no more inconvenient than a fly. "Just buy a new one."

I snorted when I realized she was right; I could afford to buy a whole wardrobe. I'd even picked up a few essentials at the transit hub, just so it wouldn't look suspicious that I was boarding without a suitcase.

If Asia noticed my light packing, she hadn't commented on it. If anything, she took it as an invitation. "I'll take you shopping tomorrow. We won't have as much time as I'd hoped, since we also have to cram in all your appointments, but we'll make it work."

She pushed her sleeve up and regarded her watch, as if that could conjure more minutes from thin air. "As soon as we land, you've got an appointment for a facial and waxing. I want you looking at least halfway decent for tomorrow's dinner—I've invited some old friends and you need to make a good impression. But we should be able to hit a couple of boutiques afterwards. We need to at least get your dress so your stylist has time to fit it."

"Sounds great," I managed with a smile that I'm sure looked as painful as it felt. The nonstop schedule sounded like torture, made worse by such sinister words as "waxing."

She was too engrossed in her digital calendar to notice. She used two pointed fingers to key commands into her watch's screen. "I'm going to see if I can move your nail appointment to Friday. Maybe I can have the jeweler pick out some pieces and deliver them instead of taking you to the gallery. That might help…"

She evidently didn't expect me to contribute to the next seventy-two hours of my life, because she bustled off without waiting for a response. I let out my breath and sank back in my seat. I had no idea being Cinderella was so exhausting.

Maybe it wouldn't be so bad if I actually *wanted* to go to the ball.

"Try to look more excited."

I started and looked up to see Jayde leering over me. He'd cleaned up well; he'd traded his fatigues for a pressed and tasseled dress uniform. With his black hat and white gloves, he looked like a proper military escort, which as far as Asia knew, that's what he was.

He bent towards me, one hand folded behind his back and the other extended. It was a polite, fluid motion—and oh so threatening. "You need to act more excited, like you can't wait to buy a new dress." His hot breath brushed my ear as he spoke in a harsh whisper. "She's going to suspect something."

I tried to squirm away from him, but there was nowhere to go; my shoulder was pressed against the window. There was already a long list of rules I had to obey if I wanted Stanyard to live: *Don't damage the implant. Don't tell anyone what you're doing. Don't mention Blue Fire.* Did I have to add "enjoy playing dress-up" to the list? "Sorry, it's hard to be excited about shoes when I'm being held at gunpoint."

He stiffened, and I knew I'd gone too far. He glanced around the cabin, but Asia had disappeared into her private room.

"Then fake it, princess," he slithered. His hand brushed aside the hem of his jacket, revealing his phone clipped to his belt. "Or I'll have to make a call."

I pinched my eyes shut and turned to the window. "Okay, okay, I will. Just please, leave me alone."

He straightened slowly, letting the threat linger, then withdrew to the other side of the cabin.

I grabbed my phone and tried to look busy—not that there was anything on it. Jayde had given me a new device so Andromeda could check in online, but he'd blocked most apps and given himself remote access. There was no way for me to call for help on this phone.

Not that there was anyone to call. Stanyard was halfway around the world being held hostage by Lev. Ephesus was on a transit to Mars, completely cut off from communication. And Nic wouldn't help me even if I could get a hold of him.

As usual, he'd been right about me. He'd been right about everything.

I'm disappointed in you, Philadelphia.

I turned the phone off and suffocated the feelings. If Jayde caught me crying, it would all be over.

I picked up my backpack—the one personal belonging I'd been able to bring—and rifled through it. I'd been allowed to keep the paper Bible Stanyard had given me—a bitter mercy. All the precious artifact did was remind me of the friend I was putting in danger and the God who had stopped talking to me.

I'd been praying fiercely all day in every spiritual and earthly language I knew. I prayed that the implant machine would malfunction, or someone would catch us in the elevator, or even that a stranger at the transit hub would recognize me and stop us. I begged God to send someone, anyone to save me.

But no one came, and the kill chip was now embedded in my palm, the scar hidden by a layer of regenerated skin. And throughout the whole process, the Holy Spirit had remained silent. I didn't get a rush of courage or any brilliant ideas; I asked for wisdom and heard nothing.

I was alone.

I shoved the Bible aside and reached to the bottom of the bag. Cold metal brushed my fingers, and I pulled the object out: the star of David pin.

I twisted it in my hand, feeling a rush of miserable anger. I thought Lev and I had a camaraderie, an understanding forged by mutual grief. We both knew what it was like to lose our families and our freedom for our faith, but apparently, he wasn't afraid to shed more blood for the cause.

"Are you all right?"

I looked up to see Asia standing next to me. I took stock of my face and realized I hadn't been doing a very good job of keeping my emotions masked. I glanced around the cabin, but thankfully Jayde wasn't in sight.

I plastered on a smile. "Just thinking about my dad." I dropped the pin in my backpack, zipped it up, and kicked it under the seat.

"I understand." Asia slid into the seat across from me and set two drinks on the table. Hers was bubbly and fancy—mine was plain black coffee.

I took it skeptically. "How did you know how I liked it?"

She winked. "You seemed like the type."

I accepted the peace offering and slipped it slowly, grateful to have something to do with my mouth other than fake a smile.

"How is your father doing?" Asia asked after I'd had a few minutes to rally my courage in my coffee.

"He's still in therapy," I said, careful to keep it vague. "But he's progressing well."

"Did you talk to him before you left?"

I didn't talk to anyone before I left. "We haven't woken him up yet," I said, swirling my mug. "Mrs. Nolan says he needs more time."

At least that was one thing I didn't have to worry about. Mrs. Nolan would take care of my dad, especially once she realized I was gone. She shouldn't let anyone touch him.

"And his memory?"

I looked up at Asia, debating how much to share. It was really none of her business, but then again, maybe it would be better if she knew Red Rain was dead. "It's gone," I whispered.

She pursed her lips. "I'm sorry," she said, voice thick with disappointment. "I can recommend some neurotherapists."

I'm sure you can. I shrugged and returned to my coffee.

She tapped her glass with her manicured fingernail. "Maybe when he's well you can both move to Beijing. We'd love to have you."

"I'm sure he'd like that," I lied, and tried not to laugh. I wouldn't be welcome in Beijing after this trip. After this mission was complete, Andromeda would be dead, just like Philadelphia was.

No, after this trip, there would be only one place I'd be welcome. Jayde claimed I could go free, but it was a technicality. We both knew there would be only one identity I could wear after I killed the General Secretary.

I am Blue Fire.

17

If Asia's itinerary sounded aggressive on paper, it was even more exhausting in practice.

Her driver met us on the runway when we landed the next day. He helped me into the car, sparing me the misery of holding Jayde's hand, and then whisked us across the city. As he navigated traffic with wizard-like efficiency, I stole my first look at China through the tinted windows. The traditional colors of gold on red blurred with the silvery-blue of glass and steel. Towering apartments pierced the clouds, while historic archways and shrines watched with shuttered eyes. Everything was splashed with neon and emblazoned with the United seal—reminding us, always, who was in control.

We soon reached downtown, where I was escorted to an exclusive spa on the top floor of a high-rise. Jayde, thankfully, was forced to wait in the lobby, but I got no reprieve as a trio of technicians set about sculpting me into a porcelain doll. Asia gave them a laundry list of specifications, like I was a sewing pattern to be stitched together. No one asked my opinion.

What was most infuriating was how little effect the procedure seemed to have. Despite all the poking and plucking and stripping and *pain* of the humiliating four-hour appointment, I came out looking exactly as I had gone in. I stared in the mirror and tried to figure out what was different, except for the fact that my eyebrows were a little thinner.

At least Asia seemed satisfied. While I was on the table, she'd taken it upon herself to pick out my dinner outfit: a ruffled blouse and pleated ocher skirt, paired with a lavender blazer that I'm sure was the height of fashion somewhere. I felt like a quaint schoolgirl, especially next to her with her deadly heels and immaculate white suit.

She hustled me across town to an opulent restaurant, where she introduced me to a dozen people as affluent and terrifying as she. There was a mix of native elites and imported American and European politicians, all of which had names and titles I'd never remember. But they all had one thing in common: They were dripping with praises about how *thrilled* they were to meet me. They slathered me with condolences over Thames's death and gushed about how lucky I was to have been plucked from the trenches, each of them offering to introduce me to this or that activity or take me on this or that outing.

I forced a pretty smile, repeating platitudes about how honored I was to be here. But inwardly, each benevolent smile and patronizing pat on the arm had me recoiling in disgust. This was why I'd never wanted to become a Nolan, why I never wanted to go with Asia: I didn't want to be a trophy.

At least no one expected a trophy to do anything but smile and nod. The rules of etiquette were simple, as Asia had reminded me repeatedly on the ride over:

Speak only when spoken to.

And if someone does not offer you their hand, bow.

Almost everyone that night offered me their hand. I accepted each unspoken invitation of friendship, struggling not to think about the bomb in my palm. I reminded myself over and over that it would only trigger for the intended target, but that didn't stop my hand from sweating or my fingers from shaking. Thankfully, everyone thought my nervousness was charming, and the meal passed without incident. Even Jayde gave my performance a pass.

By the time we'd finished dessert, I was dead on my feet. But Asia would not be deterred from her schedule, and she dragged me to a boutique where each price tag had more zeros than I could count. I'm not sure why I needed to be there, because unsurprisingly, Asia had already conjured a precise picture of the dress I should wear to the gala. All I did was sit on the velvet ottoman, sipping metallic sparkling water and trying to avoid my reflection in the octagonal mirrors that turned the fitting room into a horror funhouse.

After a dozen styles were brought and refused, Asia finally allowed me to try one on. The clerks helped me slip into the sheath of black velvet, then put me on a stool so they could fiddle with the hemline. I finally looked my reflection in the eye and tried to decide if I liked who I saw.

To her credit, Asia had picked out an understated, if not demure, gown. It was modeled after a qipao, with a starched collar, three-quarter sleeves, and a flared skirt with a slit to the knee. The black velvet was embedded with tiny crystals, making it look like the dress had been dipped in starlight. It was pretty, to be sure, but it looked like something Asia would wear.

I suppose that was her intent.

It was long past dark by the time we made the trek back to the Nolan estate. The city glowed in technicolor, but I was too exhausted to appreciate it. I could only hope Asia had reached the end of her itinerary, and I could put a closed door between me and Jayde.

I jerked out of my stupor when the car rocked to a stop in front of the most magnificent house I had ever seen. In fact, calling it a house seemed like an insult: It looked like a tiny palace. It was modeled after a traditional villa, with a two-story ring of rooms framing a private courtyard. The walls were made of stone so pale it appeared to glow in the moonlight, and the black-tiled roof was sloped and capped with statues of dragons. Giant iron phoenixes stood guard on either side of the front door, their flared wings sweeping up to the sky.

"Gorgeous, isn't it? Some of the masonry is original." Asia brushed past where I stood gawking on the sidewalk and led the way through the gate.

I followed her gingerly, almost afraid to put my feet on the sparkling tile walkway. "I get to stay here?"

"Stay here?" Asia cackled. She stopped on the top step and looked back at me. "Darling, you *own* this house."

I gaped at her.

She gestured at the keypad next to the door. "Try it."

I slowly climbed the steps, casting a nervous glance up at the massive phoenixes. They glared down at me with carved eyes as I passed under their wings, and I briefly wondered if they were about to come alive and devour me for being an imposter.

I cautiously approached the door and pressed my thumb to the keypad. It chirped and flashed green.

Asia echoed the sentiment as she pushed the door open. "Welcome home, Andromeda."

I stepped into the entryway and was taken aback by the sudden shift in aesthetic. Where the exterior of the home was traditional, the interior was egregiously Western. It was minimalistic to a fault, with glaring white space and blank walls. Everything was white and black and clean and sharp, with square corners and harsh edges. The only warmth in the entire space was the massive fireplace that formed the wall straight ahead, its silent flame flickering a gas-fed blue.

"Nolan Xiaojie." A posh voice and soft footsteps greeted me. I looked up to see a butler approach. He matched the aesthetic of the house perfectly, with his crisp white-and-black uniform and plastered hair. He stopped in front of me and bowed. "Peng Bai, houseman."

"Pleased to meet you," I said, and hoped that was somewhere on the scale of polite behavior.

He smiled. "It is my pleasure to make sure your estate runs smoothly. Please, if you require anything, simply say the word and I will be happy to assist."

"Thank you," I managed, and was surprised when my voice shook. Did this all really belong to me? Money was one thing, but *servants*? Is this who I was now? I fiddled with the hem of my jacket, suddenly feeling very small in my childish pleated skirt.

Thankfully, Asia had no trouble assuming command. "Peng, will you see to it that Andromeda's baggage is taken up? And show the lieutenant to the servants' quarters."

I glanced back to where Jayde waited in the doorway. He stepped forward. "I would prefer to stay close to Miss—"

"I said," Asia sneered without even looking back, "will you show the lieutenant to the *servants'* quarters?"

Jayde flushed almost as red as his hair. He stiffened and looked prepared to mouth off—then changed his mind. He gave a curt half-bow. "Goodnight, Miss Nolan." Then he shot me a glare that only I could interpret and followed Peng out of the room.

"I could have him hanged if you'd like."

I started and looked at Asia. "What?"

She tapped her lip with a pointed fingernail. "He's such a drag. I'm this close to having him arrested just to watch him squirm."

I gaped at her.

She laughed disarmingly. "It was a joke, darling. But do let me know if he's bothering you. Remember, there's nothing money and a well-placed phone call can't fix."

I frowned. She certainly didn't sound like she was joking—and part of me wished she wasn't.

She didn't give me time to contemplate the implications. "Well, don't just stand there—come see your room." She clipped towards the stairs, her heels popping sharply on the tile floor, and I hastened to follow.

She led me up the spiral staircase and down the hall to a double door that was nearly as big as the front entrance. She grabbed both handles and threw them wide open, revealing a bedroom set in the stars.

A mural of screens paneled one wall, displaying a softly moving image of a purple-blue nebula. In the middle of the room sat a massive four-poster bed piled high with blankets and pillows in varying shades of plum and navy. A fur rug softened the gray wood floor, and the furniture was a mix of mahogany and stained birch. Above it all hung a net of fairy lights that was strung from the ceiling like a constellation.

It certainly looked like a room belonging to someone named Andromeda.

"I hope you don't mind, I had it decorated," Asia said from behind me. "I thought you might find it more inviting."

"Yes," I said, and meant it. I took a slow step into the room, my shoes sinking into the plush carpet.

"One of the staff will come get you when it's time for breakfast. Be ready to leave by 8 A.M.—we've got a full day of appointments, and you need to meet with your stylist."

The thought of another day of beauty appointments filled me with dread, but I forced a nod.

"Call me if you need anything—I'm only minutes away." Asia grabbed the handles and started to close the door, then stopped. "It's good to have you home. You deserve this."

Do I? I scanned the room and tried to understand what I had done to earn this. The only reason my name was on the deed was because Thames had chosen me—and I still didn't fully understand why.

Asia didn't expect an answer. She gave me one more smile— softer, kinder this time. "Goodnight, Andromeda," she said, and closed the door.

I waited until her footsteps had faded before venturing further into the room. It was huge; the entire first floor of our old home in the containment camp would have fit inside. To the right, a mirrored hallway led to a gigantic closet and in-suite bathroom. Straight ahead, solid glass doors opened to a private balcony that overlooked the courtyard.

I stepped out into the warm night air and looked around the yard—*my* yard. More balconies lined the upper floor of the square pavilion, although all the other bedrooms were dark, curtains drawn. Below, iron statues and exotic plants decorated the stone patio that surrounded an Olympic-sized pool. The immaculate water reflected the starless night sky, the moon balanced perfectly on the still surface.

Gripping the railing, I stared at the glassy water and wished, for the very first time, that I could live here forever. I didn't even know how to comprehend such wealth. It was one thing to have enough money to buy what I needed—*this* was luxury I couldn't have dreamed up had I tried.

Of course, it would all vanish Saturday night when I shook the General's hand and ruined Andromeda's reputation.

Unless...

I told Asia what was going on.

I sank down on the ground and leaned my head against the railing, using the cool stone to center my swirling thoughts. Asia had teasingly said she could take care of Jayde, and I believed her. She practically owned the government and had unlimited resources; with one phone call she could put Jayde away *and* get Staryard to safety. No one had to die.

But I would have to tell her that I'd been planning to kill her father.

How would she react? A normal person would have me arrested, but Asia had proven herself to be anything but normal. She knew all my identities and had every reason to order my execution, but she hadn't for her own mysterious reasons. She'd made it clear that she was prepared to ignore the crimes of Blue Fire and Philadelphia Smyrna if I would only agree to be Andromeda Nolan.

No, based on her behavior tonight, I had every reason to believe that if I told Asia what was going on, she would make it all go away.

I traced the ornate pattern on the railing with my finger. All I had to do was say the word, and she'd remove Jayde. She'd have my record expunged and overturn the warrants for my father's arrest; he wouldn't even need a new file. She would get Stanyard, Tower, and Mrs. Nolan to safety. Then we could all move to Beijing. We could live behind this iron gate, watched over by carved dragons, and forget the containment camps, forget the rebellion.

And I would become Andromeda Nolan forever.

I rubbed my palm, feeling the chip flex beneath the surface. Maybe Asia was right. Maybe I was one of them.

18

It turned out Peng wasn't the only servant at my command. I was woken by a maid barely older than myself who asked if I wanted help getting ready. Thankfully, she took no for an answer.

I almost regretted sending her away when I stumbled into the closet and discovered that it was crammed full of clothes, all of which were miraculously my size. Why Asia thought I needed to go shopping was beyond me; someone had clearly gone to a lot of trouble to build a wardrobe for me. I didn't dare ask whether that person was Asia or Thames.

I rifled through the hangers until I found something that looked like it cost less than a thousand dollars. I didn't waste too much time on my appearance and threw on a minimal amount of makeup. There was no point when Asia was going to have it all redone anyway.

I went downstairs and wandered around until I found the right kitchen (there were three), where a chef had gone overboard preparing breakfast. He was French and seemed over the moon to have someone to cook for. He served me an elegantly layered bowl that was probably the most nutritious thing I'd eaten all year.

I dared to ask about Jayde and was more than a little gratified to hear he'd been served with the rest of the staff.

Asia kept her word and pulled up promptly at eight. She whisked me away to another two-hour torture session, followed by a nail appointment where it took a suspiciously long time just to give me plain white French tips. By then it was supposedly lunch time, even though I was still full from breakfast, followed by coffee, which I was more amicable towards.

At long last, it was finally time to go see my fabled stylist. The driver pulled up to a classy all-glass building in an artsy part of town. The massive front windows revealed a gaudy array of dresses, all edgy styles clearly designed to provoke. The neon sign was written in Mandarin characters, and the doorbell trilled zither music as we entered.

The lobby was empty. The place had the aura of a spa, with an abundance of potted plants and a waterfall concealing the entire back wall. I scanned the empty salon chairs while Asia rang the bell impatiently.

There was a muffled shout from somewhere in the back. Footsteps approached, followed immediately by a screeched, "What in the *world* did you do to your hair?"

I turned around to find Narissa glaring at me.

I blinked to recalibrate my reality, then realized that I shouldn't be surprised. After all, Narissa had known Thames; he'd hired her to be my stylist back when we were on Mars. She'd since changed her hairstyle to a daring asymmetrical pixie cut, but otherwise, she looked exactly like she had when I'd met her. Her simple black outfit and sharp winged eyeliner gave her a fierce elegance as she scrutinized me with palpable distaste.

"Hello again," I offered.

She didn't return the greeting. "Some nerve you have coming in here with *that* haircut," she hissed. "I tried to get you to cut your hair, but *no!* And now look at you. What even is this?"

She strode up to me and grabbed chunks of my hair with both hands, holding them out from my head.

"It was necessary," I confessed.

"It was necessary when I wanted to do it!" She growled like a cat.

"Can you fix it?" Asia asked.

"Fix it? No, the only way to fix this crime against humanity would be to shave it all off and start over."

I swallowed.

"But…" Narissa sighed and dropped my hair. "If I add some toner and lowlights, I can make her presentable."

I spread my hands. "That's why I hired the best."

Narissa finally shifted her gaze from my hair to my eyes and smiled.

"This will also need to be fitted." Asia laid a dress bag on the counter. "And her makeup will need to be—"

Narissa cut her off with a flick of her hand. "Trust me, I know all about making this one look like something she's not. I'll handle it."

Asia seemed a bit miffed to have been interrupted, but she deferred with a nod. "We'll be back to pick you up for dinner, Andromeda." Another tinkle of zither music escorted her out the door as she left.

"Andromeda, huh?" Narissa picked at her lip. "So you did decide to take the old man's name."

I looked back up at her. "Didn't really have a choice."

Something close to a smile pinched her face. "At least tell me you've been conditioning."

I shrugged sheepishly.

She rolled her eyes and grabbed the dress bag off the counter. "Well, we've got work to do. This way."

She walked to the back of the store. I followed her around the waterfall to a hidden elevator, where we descended two floors below.

The doors slid open to reveal an underground studio lit as bright as daylight. Seamless screens wrapped the entire room; the image slowly shifted between different patterns and textures, all in shades of crimson. The floor was cluttered with a drafting board, cutting table, and half a dozen headless mannequins. But the crown jewel was a gigantic dress fabricator.

It was almost as tall as I was, and it had more wires and flashing displays than Dad's cryogenics tube. In the central chamber, multiple robotic arms flashed in and out, stabbing needles and weaving threads. I walked up and watched in fascination as the bodice of a dress began to form on the table. The robotic fingers wove each line of thread, conforming the bust to some invisible pattern, almost as if the dress were being conjured out of thin air.

I breathed a sound of admiration. "Can it sew anything?"

"As long as I can dream up the pattern. It takes my sketches and turns them into a 3D model that I can tweak, then it fabricates the garment from scratch." Narissa held up a tablet with a half-finished sketch on the screen. She tossed it aside and laid the dress bag out on the cutting table. "Now, what did you bring me?"

There was the sound of a zipper opening, and Narissa retched.

I glanced back. "Asia picked it out."

"I can see that." Narissa pinched a chunk of the sparkly fabric between two fingertips, as if she were afraid it was going to bite her. "No, no—you're not wearing this."

Then she scooped it up, bag and all, and tossed it on a pile of forgotten fabric.

"But—"

"First of all, that'll make you look like you're forty-five. Second of all..." She turned back to me and hesitated, the light shifting behind her eyes. "It doesn't really scream... revolution, does it?"

I stiffened.

She shrugged. "I know what's going on. I was there when it started."

I looked into her eyes and waited.

She took a deep, rallying breath. "You're not here just to attend a party, are you?"

I took a step back. "I can't—"

"No, no." She put her hands up. "Don't tell me. I don't want to know. I just need to know how high to make the slit. Are you going to be running?"

I never should have stopped running. "No," I admitted. That was what made the whole plan so sinister: All I would be doing was shaking someone's hand.

"Good, that gives me options. Up." She gestured at a stool that stood against the back wall.

I kicked off my shoes and obeyed, stepping on the stool and standing up straight. Narissa took one slow lap around me, eyes scanning up and down while she muttered to herself.

After she'd been computing in silence for a long moment, I ventured, "Why are you helping—"

"I said I don't want to know," she snapped. She straightened and glanced around the room. "This color is all wrong though. I need... blue."

At her command, the screens on the wall shifted to display a gradient of royal blue textures. Narissa shook her head. "Too bright. Try... periwinkle."

The screens flickered again. "Nope, too purple. Maybe... slate."

The image changed one more time. This time, a roulette of storm clouds, deep water, and quartz painted the whole room a muted gray blue.

"Much better." Narissa took a step back and eyed me from a distance. "You're about a twenty-seven and a quarter inch waist, right?"

I flushed self-consciously. "How did you..."

She glanced around the room, as if verifying that we were alone. Then she reached up and popped her contacts out. Blinking, she looked back up at me, revealing two eyes that weren't human at all.

Two robotic orbs sat where her eyes should have been. They looked like miniature computers suspended in glass marbles. The artificial lenses focused on me while the microscopic motherboards flickered with an unintelligible readout.

"You're… blind?" I finally managed.

She nodded. "With special glasses, I could see a little, but not enough to do what I really wanted." She reached out and fingered the fabric that was draped over the chair next to her. "My parents tried every surgery they could afford, but it wasn't enough to get me into design school. Every time I tried to apply for a grant or enter my dresses in a competition, they denied me."

Her artificial gaze shifted back to me. "The United doesn't like imperfect people any more than it likes religious brats."

I knew that was true.

She looked down, rolling her contacts around in her fingers. "Then, one day, I hear about this new program. The government was giving away implants—*free*—to anyone who needed them. I could have brand-new augmented eyesight, completely paid for by the United."

She laughed suddenly, the sound shattered and cruel. "Unfortunately, I failed to read the terms and conditions."

I connected the dots. "Can they…"

She tipped her head back and slid her contacts in, blinking and rolling her eyes until they adjusted. "The government can hear everything I hear and see everything I see. That's why I say… I really *don't* want to know."

I instinctively grabbed my upper arm, where my thunderbird tattoo was hidden under my shirt and a bandage.

"Don't worry," she assured, "I doubt anyone's listening. I haven't caused trouble in a long time. But if I were to say the wrong thing—say, the callsign of a certain revolutionary figure—it might trip the algorithm."

I nodded rapidly, feeling all the dread and fear slip to my stomach.

"It has its perks, though," Narissa said, her cheerfulness salted with pain. "I can take measurements, send sketches to my machine, even ask the computer to match your foundation shade. And it's not like it pops up in the corner of my vision like a stupid visor—I just *know*."

A little sense of wonder found its way into my consciousness. "I assume it wasn't hard to get into design school."

"Top of my class. And—I didn't have to sign the file."

"What?"

She picked up a tablet and started sketching. "They don't do files here—that's an American thing. You people like choice, so they let you pick what kind of government control you want."

I'd never thought of it that way, but I realized, with a sickening weight in my chest, that she was right. You could choose to assimilate and obey the rules of the system, or you could live in a containment camp under complete surveillance. Either way the government was in control. Either way the United won.

And apparently, we could accept that as long as we got to sign off on it.

"Here, we prefer more fashionable solutions. There's thirty million people in this province alone—we don't have time to be checking people's paperwork. No, we let the computer do the heavy lifting." She tapped the side of her head with her stylus. "I don't need a piece of paper to tell me where I can and cannot go when the algorithm will let the boss know if I get out of line."

I rubbed my arm. "Can they… shut it down remotely?"

"Probably," she muttered in a tone that suggested she'd spent years convincing herself not to think about it.

I started to pray for her, then realized I had no idea what to even ask for. The only thing worse than a prison was one you carried around with you.

She set the tablet down and grabbed a remnant of chiffon. "Everyone gets to pick their chains, Andromeda." She started circling me again, bunching the fabric in different ways to see how it hung on my frame. "Be careful which ones you choose."

I held my arms out and let her work as I chewed on her words. All my life, I'd chosen to be unassimilated—to live at the bottom of society so I could salvage some semblance of autonomy. But if I stayed in Beijing, I'd be trading all of that for another containment camp. This one had a chef and a butler and a pool, but it was a containment camp nonetheless. The Nolan estate was a prison—it would only protect me so long as I played the role of Andromeda. If I failed to follow the rules, if I failed to be the perfect daughter Asia wanted me to be, the system would kick me out.

Narissa was right—Andromeda was just another set of chains. Was she the chains I wanted?

19

"Open your eyes."

I hesitated, almost afraid of what I would see. It was Saturday afternoon, and I'd spent the entire day in a chair at Narissa's salon. She salvaged my hair, adding toner and lowlights to bring some warmth back into the bleached locks. She fixed my hack job by meticulously scissoring in layers, then twisted my hair up and clipped on an extension to give me an elegant curled updo. Then she spent an hour painting on my face, each stroke of contour and eyeliner done with precision.

At long last, she had me stand on a stool and told me to close my eyes while she helped me into the dress. I felt the rustle of cool silk slide over my arms and suddenly felt exposed and unprotected. I was walking into the most dangerous party of my life, intent on starting a war, and I was wearing heels and had bare shoulders.

"You can look now."

I swallowed, opened my eyes, and stared at the woman in the mirror.

The dress was a barely-there pale blue that seemed to shift in and out of gray, like the underside of a cloud. The boned bodice was understated, with ruched cap sleeves that just grazed my shoulders. But where the bodice was reserved, the skirt was captivating. Layers of sheer chiffon flowed off the waist. Hidden on the second and third layers was a bold network of silver embroidery. The lines were jagged and random, making it look like the skirt was made from shattered glass. When I moved, the metallic thread flashed in and out of the light, like lightning flickering behind the clouds.

I was a thunderbird.

I looked down at Narissa. "But why…"

She finished adjusting the hem and straightened. "I figured if you were going to make a scene tonight… you needed to dress the part."

She offered her hand and helped me down from the stool. I squeezed her fingers, a wave of guilt crashing into my mind. "But what about you? If they find out who made this dress…"

"Oh, they'll know." She reached up and adjusted my sleeve. Only a thin layer of fabric covered my tattoo today, because soon there would be no reason to hide it. If I went through with this, one fatal handshake would turn me into a war hero. On live TV, I would initiate the revolution—and become Blue Fire forever. And I'm sure the government would not be thrilled with the designer who had turned me into the thunderbird.

"But I can't… I won't be able to protect you," I managed. *"They'll kill you,"* was the truth I was too afraid to say.

Her cold hands grazed my skin as she clipped the strand of pearls Asia had given me around my neck. She stepped back and met my eyes in the mirror, hers blinking and unafraid. "Do what you came to do."

Jayde was waiting on the bench outside the salon in full regalia. He stood up when I exited, his eyes taking in my dress as the embroidery crackled in the sunlight. I could tell the meaning of the design was not lost on him when he grinned.

He bowed and offered his hand. I took it and allowed him to assist me into the car, but only because the driver was watching.

Asia had said she would meet us at the party, so she sent a pearl white stretch limo to chauffeur us around—an excess, as usual. Despite the fact that the car could have seated twenty, Jayde sat uncomfortably close to me on the padded leather bench. He asked the driver to turn up the music, then leaned and whispered in my ear.

"The party will be spread out all across the compound. There will be food in the Hall of Dispelling Clouds by the docks, and the General Secretary will be taking visitors in the Tower of Incense, which is in the middle of the complex. Everyone who's invited to the party gets a chance to meet the General, but you have to wait to be called. When it's your turn, if Asia has done her job, he'll want to shake your hand."

I instinctively rubbed my palm.

Jayde grabbed my wrist to stop me. "You can do this. I know you don't see yourself as a leader, but I still believe in you."

"It's too late for camaraderie." I yanked my hand from his grasp.

"Then just follow my lead." He adjusted his white gloves. "As soon as the deed is done, there will be chaos. I've got several friends at the party; one of them is going to grab you and take you to safety. Stick to the plan and you'll make it out alive."

I nodded and scooted away from him down the bench. It wasn't me I was worried about. Jayde had made it abundantly clear that Lev would be watching the party on TV. If I did not shake the General's hand, Stanyard would die.

One way or another, I was going to murder someone tonight. The question was who.

The sun was just beginning to set when we joined the long line of cars entering the outer grounds of the Summer Palace. All the VIPs, of which I apparently was one, were being escorted over the Bridge of Seventeen Arches and ferried across the lake so they could get a full view of the palace. The vast complex was lit with hundreds of lanterns, making it look like the hills were blanketed in fireflies. The descending sun turned the lake to blood as we docked and were escorted through the arch into the first courtyard.

The stone pavilion was crammed with affluence. A mix of Western ball gowns and Eastern qipaos mingled with suits and ties. Live musicians played traditional instruments while the guests kept time with their laughter. Lanterns drifted from every tree branch, and fires burned in ornate kilns. The kilns were filled with incense to keep the bugs at bay, blanketing the entire courtyard in perfume.

And everywhere there were cameras and press, capturing the entire party on film.

The Hall of Dispelling Clouds was straight ahead. The brilliant red-and-gold structure was decorated with ornate carvings and luscious calligraphy. Light poured out of the geometric windows, and the smell of decadent food floated from the open doors.

Jayde hooked his arm with mine and guided me towards the steps. "Do you want something to eat?"

"No" would have been the truthful answer; I was sure that if I tried to cram food into my clenched stomach, I would vomit. But I would rather hold chopsticks than Jayde's hand, so I nodded and followed him into the hall.

Inside, a table as nearly as long as the building was burdened with delicacies. I allowed Jayde to play the gentleman and serve me. I accepted the small plate he handed to me and tried to rally the courage to eat it.

Thankfully, I was spared the misery when someone called my name. "Andromeda!"

I looked up to see a couple approach. "I'm so glad you made it! It's great to see you again," the man said. He was American—Southern, specifically—and I loosely recognized him as someone who had been at dinner the first night.

I gratefully handed my plate back to Jayde so I could offer the man a bow.

"Oh please, none of that. You're a friend of the family." He grasped both of my hands in his and pumped them warmly. "I was telling Ivy all about you—wasn't I, honey?"

"Yes, he was! I'm so thrilled to meet you." The lustrous woman at his side let go of his arm to reach for me. I offered her a handshake, but she forwent that and came in for a hug and a kiss on the cheek instead. I was too stunned to refuse or reciprocate the gesture.

Vaguely, I registered the flash of a camera in the background as some insolent press member captured this momentous moment in time.

The woman held me at arm's length and admired me. "And look at this dress! Aren't you stunning? Thames undersold how beautiful you were."

Thames thought I was pretty? I tried to grasp the thought and gave up.

"Come on, you simply must meet the Yangs." The woman grabbed my hand and dragged me across the room, where the whole process of gushing handshakes and hugs was repeated, punctuated by the ever-present flicker of cameras. This went on for the next hour until I could have sworn I'd met everyone in the complex and had my picture taken a hundred times.

Everyone, it seemed, had heard about me from someone. Many of them were friends of Asia, but several said they'd heard about me from Thames. Apparently, Mr. and Mrs. Nolan had been talking about me since I'd moved to camp; some of these people claimed they'd been waiting to meet me for years.

I told them I was flattered, and my surprise was genuine. There was nothing special about me, or at least there hadn't been when Thames had met me. What had he seen in me?

Too bad I would never get to ask.

Unfortunately, tonight my fame would be a curse. If everyone else at the party had heard of me, surely the General Secretary had as well. And that was not good news.

My worst fears were confirmed when a smartly dressed guard interrupted us. "Beg pardon, Miss Nolan, but General Secretary Mong would see you."

20

The noise of the party died away as my vision flashed black.

Oh God, help.

Jayde hooked his arm through my elbow before I could even think about resisting. The guard led us out of the hall and across the courtyard to the winding stone steps that led up to the Tower of Incense. It was an agonizingly long climb that only gave me more time to panic. Each step reminded me that it was too late to turn back, and each step brought me closer to my death.

No matter what I chose, part of me would not leave that building. Either Andromeda would die, or Blue Fire would.

Finally, we reached the top. The three-story tower loomed over the pavilion, its octagonal eaves strung with lanterns and banners bearing the United seal. The most privileged of the guests decorated the patio, and every three steps was another guard, several of which exchanged subtle nods with Jayde. All eyes were on me as I was escorted up the stairs and into the building.

The tower had once been a temple, but the religious artifacts had long since been stripped away and the first floor repaneled into a throne room of sorts. Guests and guards milled around the perimeter and supplied the ambiance while butlers ferried drinks. In the center of it all, General Secretary Mong stood on a raised platform, receiving guests in a line.

He was not a large man, which was somehow all the more threatening. His hair was feathered with a proud gray, and his face was folded in a practiced smile. The way he carried himself reminded me of Thames: Everything about his movements was calm, if not understated, and yet he projected a power that formed the center of gravity in the room.

He was flanked by several guards, all of whom were bejeweled with military medals, and his top staff. Asia stood a few feet away to his left. She spotted me as we entered. I saw her eyes scan my dress, face contorted in confusion. But then her expression lit up and she grinned, broad and catlike.

Jayde tugged on my arm. I followed his gaze to the side of the room, where a cluster of press people manned a camera. I heard the reporter quietly narrating each introduction, inflating the egos of each guest as they passed in front of the General.

"Everyone is watching," Jayde whispered, as if I needed to be told. "As soon as you shake his hand, the war for freedom starts."

Yes, I'll start a war—but will it bring freedom?

As if sensing my hesitation, Jayde laid his hand over mine. "You can do this." I looked into his eyes and saw that they were wide, genuine. "I believe in you, Blue Fire."

He did—he really did. I could tell by his excited, hopeful expression. He truly believed this was the right thing to do.

But did I?

God—Jesus—what do I do? I mentally cried, fighting to get the prayer out through the whirlwind of doubts and fears.

The silence in my soul was deafening.

The line shifted forward. I looked ahead and watched as the General received the next guest. A guard introduced the woman at the head of the line, and then the General judged her. I saw the General weigh the lady's life in the scales with a single glance. Then, after a moment's hesitation, he offered her his hand. She accepted it with gushing praises. A couple of pleasantries were exchanged, and then the woman was shuffled away to make room for the next guest, who was not so lucky. The foreign diplomat behind her received only a nod in greeting. He bowed shakily and scuttled away.

And then, as if time had skipped forward, it was my turn.

I reflexively lifted the hem of my skirt as Jayde helped me onto the platform. He let go of my arm and melted into the crowd, leaving me alone with the General and my screaming thoughts.

Asia winked at me in silent welcome and beckoned me forward. My ears rang as I approached the General. The click of my heels on the wooden floor sounded like gunfire—could everyone else hear them?

Vaguely, I registered that someone was introducing me. "Nolan Xiaojie."

I froze.

The General glanced at me. He spared me only a breath—the briefest pause in his sentence—before turning back to the man at his side and continuing his conversation.

Hope fluttered through me. I meant nothing to him. Maybe—maybe he didn't want to shake my hand. This could all be avoided if he didn't offer me his hand. *Thank you, Jesus—*

Suddenly, Asia touched her father's arm and leaned towards his ear. "This is the girl I told you about. This is Thames's daughter."

The conversation stopped, and so did my heart.

The General turned back to me and gave me a second look. His eyes lit up. "Ahh! So this is Andromeda."

The attention of everyone in the room shifted to me. I heard whispers in the background and saw the camera lens focus and knew the entire world was watching.

The General smiled. "It's an honor to finally meet you."

And then he offered his hand.

At that moment, the God who had been quiet for so long rushed in my ear.

For such a time as this.

I stared at the General's hand as mine instinctively slid forward.

And then I grabbed my skirt and bowed.

"The honor is all mine," I said, and was surprised when my voice came out clear and strong.

Yes, God had made me Andromeda Nolan for a reason. But this was not it.

Someone gasped. I looked up and realized it was Asia. She'd gone as pale as her Chinese complexion would allow. And then, suddenly, the color came rushing back into her expression as she glared at me, her eyes filled with disgust. Several people around us muttered in surprise.

I swallowed. Had I violated some unspoken rule of etiquette? Was I about to be executed for refusing the General's handshake? I hadn't planned on making it out of this party alive, but being beheaded for social ineptitude hadn't been on the list of options.

The General, however, seemed unoffended. He laughed, his grin cracking the sides of his face, as he slid his hand to its neutral position behind his back. "Such a polite young woman. Thames taught you well."

I donned my prettiest smile as I straightened. "He always wanted the best for me."

It was my turn to look surprised. Where had that come from? The words were graceful, elegant—and they weren't even a lie.

"That he did. I want you to know that I am deeply sorry for your family's loss." The General dipped his head in condolence. "How are you handling it?"

Did he want an honest answer to that question? The look in his eyes said yes, but I couldn't imagine why he cared. I glanced at the people standing nearby, searching for a social clue, but everyone just seemed surprised that the General and I were even having a conversation. Even Asia couldn't seem to recalibrate as she glanced back and forth between her father and me, her brow knotted.

After taking a breath to check my tone of voice, I gave him a modified story. "It's been difficult these past few days, sir, seeing the house, the wardrobe, the staff—everything he meant for me to have."

His smile returned, gentler this time. "It's your first time in Beijing, isn't it?" When I nodded, he winked. "Feeling a bit overwhelmed by it all?"

A beautiful laugh bubbled out of my throat before I could stop it. "In the best way possible, sir."

He echoed the sound. "I can only imagine. Have you thought about moving back here? We'd love to have you and your mother nearby."

His tone of voice suggested that he genuinely meant that, so I gave him the answer he wanted to hear. "After seeing the pool in the backyard, I don't think I have a choice."

That time, even some of his advisors laughed. He smiled benevolently at them, as if soaking up their mirth, before turning back to me. "I know what you mean. I've been there several times."

"We—I—would love to have you visit again. It would be my deepest honor to serve you."

The collective breath left the crowd again. Asia looked mortified, if not a little impressed. I resisted the urge to clutch my throat as I tried to figure out where the audacious words had come from.

Did I just invite the General over for dinner?

I couldn't even remember thinking the words; they just rolled off my lips as fluidly as a prayer.

And that's when I recognized that it wasn't me speaking.

Do not worry about what to say or how to say it. At that time you will be given what to say.

The smile remained on the General's face—poised and powerful—as he weighed me with his gaze. After a moment, he bent forward in a bow. "I would be delighted to receive your invitation."

And he just accepted?

I picked up my skirt and dipped as low as I could. "Thank you for honoring my family in this way."

A murmur erupted from the bystanders, and I caught several envious glances being shot in my direction. I twisted my skirt in my fingers as a new feeling of power rippled down my nerves.

I am Andromeda Nolan. And this is how I will fight my war.

The General started to say something else, but one of his advisors leaned over and whispered in his ear. He rolled his eyes. "It's always something. My apologies, Andromeda, but I must step away. Once you've chosen a date, forward the details to my daughter—she knows my calendar." He gestured at Asia, who recovered from her shock long enough to nod politely.

I bowed one more time for good measure. "Thank you for speaking with me, your excellence."

I turned to see Jayde standing at the edge of the platform, holding out his hand. His expression was unreadable.

Panic immediately displaced the feeling of victory in my head as I mechanically offered him my arm and let him help me off the platform. *Oh Jesus, protect me now.*

"The pleasure was all mine. I hope to see you again very soon," the General said as he allowed his advisors to herd him away. "Oh, and Andromeda…"

Jayde froze, his fingers pinching my arm. I glanced back.

A strange light glinted behind the General's eyes. "Next time I offer you my hand… don't refuse it."

I swallowed. "Of course, sir."

He disappeared into the crowd as the motion of the party resumed. Asia gave me one last stare as she hustled after her father.

Jayde pushed me towards the side of the room. His entire body was taut as he struggled to conceal his anger. "I hope you enjoyed your little *chat* with the General," he hissed in my ear, and then spat something very foul.

The adrenaline returned, bringing a wave of fear crashing down. I saw the hate burning in Jayde's eyes and knew I had only moments before my world ended. What would happen to Stanyard? My dad? What about the rebellion? What about—

And then I remembered Narissa's confident indifference in the face of death, and I finally understood.

I sucked in a breath and centered myself around the truth that my dad had failed to find: It was God's job to protect my family. It was my job to do what was right.

I found my courage and my voice. "Jayde, listen. You don't—"

"Shut up," he hissed, and pulled me towards the stairwell. One of his associates was there waiting. With a glance around at the crowd, he swiped his thumb on the panel and let us in.

The door slammed behind us, plunging us into the near darkness of the unused stairwell. I tripped on my skirt twice as Jayde hauled me up the stairs. "Jayde, stop!"

"You don't get to call the shots anymore." With a final yank, he pushed me through the door at the top of the stairs. I stumbled out into the warm night air and realized we were on the third floor.

Jayde slammed the door and advanced towards me. "You had one job."

I glanced around, but there was nowhere to go on the narrow balcony. This floor wasn't open to the public, so there was no one in sight. I could hear the laughter of people in the courtyard far below.

"Go ahead, scream," Jayde threatened, his words slurred with rage.

I swallowed and contemplated doing just that.

"They'll never make it in time." He reached into the folds of his uniform and pulled out a knife, flicking it open. I slid back and rammed into the railing. Against my better judgment, I turned and looked down.

It was a three-story drop to the stone courtyard below.

I gripped the railing as my courage buckled. It wouldn't be the first time I'd fallen from a great height. But this time, there would be nothing to break my fall.

"Jayde," I panted, trying and failing to find the peace I'd had moments before. "Please."

He shook his head. "Do you have any idea how much damage you've done? You missed the signal. You failed! And because of you, Operation Thunderbird never happened. It's going to take me years to build back what we had!"

He lurched forward and slammed into my shoulder. A scream died in my throat as I almost flipped backward over the railing, but he grabbed my arm and held me down. I hyperventilated as the world spun.

His hand closed around my throat, cutting off my airflow. His breath burned hot on my ear as he growled, "I do hope the people love a martyr, because that's what you're about to be."

He pressed the blade of his knife to my chin, and I closed my eyes. *Jesus, save me.*

"Well, that's just rude."

Jayde jerked back. My world stopped and restarted as I recognized the voice.

"Nic!"

He came around the corner of the balcony, clearly dressed for the occasion. He wore a white suit jacket paired with black pants and a smart bowtie, and a single red rose was clipped to his lapel.

"Sorry to intrude on your emasculated display of power." He regarded Jayde as if he were the worm inside of an apple. "But I believe she promised me the next set."

Jayde contorted his face. "Q? What are you—"

Nic put his finger up. "First of all, that's Dr. Von Nieuwenhuyse to you. Second of all, last I checked, I have a piece of paper stating that the woman you're about to throw off a balcony is my daughter, so frankly the rest is none of your business."

The statement was delivered with his usual dose of salt and disinterest, but his words sent relief and forgiveness rushing through me.

Nic came back for me.

Jayde recovered from the shock. "How charming," he grunted. He lifted the knife. "But don't come any closer."

"And now I'm bored." Nic whipped an electric pistol from his pocket and flipped it on in one smooth motion. "I'll make the math easy for you. Let her go, and I won't shoot to kill."

Jayde didn't even blink. "Is that how you want to do it? Two can play that game."

He reached up and grabbed my styled curls, yanking my head back in a motion that was all too familiar.

But this time, I remembered.

I reached up and grasped his hand with both of mine. Hours of practice kicked in as I ducked and turned, wrenching his arm. He yelled as his wrist twisted. I broke free and ran to Nic.

He pushed me behind him, and suddenly, I knew I was safe.

Jayde gaped at me as horror washed over his expression. Then his eyes shifted to the gun, and for the first time since I'd met him, he looked afraid.

Nic clucked his tongue. "Did I say I wouldn't shoot to kill? Because I'm strongly reconsidering that position. It's something about your face."

Jayde clenched his fists and tried to regain control by raising his voice. "I have people! They're waiting for me downstairs."

"So? There's another stairwell," Nic chirped, and fired.

Bright blue electricity arced from the gun to Jayde's chest. He gasped as all the life was sucked from his lungs. He jerked once, then stumbled forward and collapsed without a sound.

I slapped a hand over my mouth. "Is he…"

Nic looked down at the settings on the gun. "Ah, what a shame, I had it on stun. He'll thank me in an hour." He powered off the weapon and concealed it in his jacket. "Let's go."

I gathered my skirt and followed him around the building to the other stairwell. My brain caught up with my new reality, and

I realized we had only minutes before Jayde's people figured out something was wrong. "Nic," I panted as we pounded down the stairs, "wait. There's something you should know—"

"I'm sure there's a lot of things. Act natural." Nic paused at the bottom of the stairs and reset his hair.

I shook my skirt out and shoved my hairpin back in. "No, listen, Stanyard—"

"Already taken care of." Nic scooped my arm in his, opened the door, and dragged me outside. The stairwell opened to the back of the porch that wrapped the tower, mercifully away from any prying camera lenses. We waited until a servant passed by with a tray of food and then followed in his wake as we walked around the building, down the steps, and merged into the crowd in the courtyard. The rhythm of the party continued undisturbed—but I knew that wouldn't last long.

I gripped Nic's arm and hoped the gesture looked elegant and not panicked. "But how—"

"I had Ephesus make the calls—everyone's fine. I sent Pizza Boy to stay with my parents. This way." Nic steered me towards the stairs that led back down the hill.

The fear that had been driving me for days evaporated, leaving me breathless. Stanyard was safe—and had been all this time. God had protected him.

Through Nic.

And Ephesus. I tried to imagine Nic and my brother working in harmony and couldn't decide which was more impressive: The fact that they'd cooperated towards a common goal, or the fact that the common goal was my safety.

Of course, the real miracle was how Nic even knew what was going on. "But how did you know he was in trouble?"

He gave an eyeroll so passionate that every muscle in his face moved. "You're not complicated, Andi. I knew that if what's-his-face back there had convinced you to go through with this against your will, then he was holding someone at gunpoint. Process of elimination suggested it was Pizza Boy."

"He's got a name," I reminded him.

"Everyone does."

I dropped the argument and struggled to keep up as he descended the stairs a little faster than was proper. The math still wasn't adding up. "How did you know I was going against my will?" I remembered our final conversation and winced. Last Nic knew, this was what I wanted.

And last I knew, he was prepared to abandon me to the consequences of my decision.

He didn't answer me until we reached the bottom of the stairs. "Mom called."

"What?"

He stopped under a tree and waited for a cluster of giggling couples to pass us. The aroma of food still soaked the air as the crowd continued to wine and dine, completely oblivious to the crisis that had just been averted.

"When you didn't show for dinner, she went up to your room and found your tablet," Nic explained. "She appropriately freaked out and called your emergency contact—me."

I felt as if I were floating as Nic guided me across the courtyard towards the docks. I could see it now—Mrs. Von's religious adherence to her schedule, the contact settings on my tablet—all the dominoes that had been put in place to save me. God *had* answered my prayer for salvation—the moment I'd asked.

And He'd sent Nic of all people.

Nic paused under the last archway and checked to make sure we were not being followed, but no one questioned our premature exit from the party. We hurried to the docks and boarded a waiting ferry. Mercifully, there were no other passengers, so we had the boat to ourselves except for the servants, who gave us a respectful berth. Nic lowered me into a seat by the stern and then sat down a comfortable distance away.

I stared at him, reliving our last conversation. I pictured his face twisted in rage, the curses flying off his lips. I remembered the hateful accusations I'd thrown at him as I tore our relationship down with my words. And I heard the hideous screech of my tablet as he blocked me and put a *"the end"* on our friendship.

I'm disappointed in you, Philadelphia.

I waited until we were almost across the lake before voicing my thoughts. "You came."

He was watching the approaching shore and didn't even turn to look at me. "Why wouldn't I come?"

"Because I…" I choked on the words, not sure which I was more afraid of: my mistakes or my feelings.

Nic had no qualms against either. "Oh, you mean because you betrayed me?"

I twisted my hands in my lap. "That's not exactly what I'd call it—"

"You betrayed me," he continued matter-of-factly. He leaned back against the railing and checked my sins off like a grocery list. "You betrayed my trust, you betrayed our friendship, you betrayed everything we ever stood for. You let me down."

There it was—the crushing rejection that took my world out from under me. The boat rocked to a stop, and he got up and started walking without even a glance at me. I hurried after him, fighting my skirts and the impending need to cry. He strode down the path to the bridge, oblivious to both.

"Nic, stop!" I gasped.

He halted, back to me.

I caught up to him and spilled my heart before he could interrupt. "If that's how you feel, then why are you helping me?"

He looked up at the night sky. "Why?"

I braced myself as the tears I'd been swallowing all evening splashed across my vision.

He finally turned and, for the first time that night, met my eyes. "Do you think I care for you so little that betraying me would make a difference?"

"I mean… yeah?" I admitted, and blushed. That is exactly what I thought.

And I'd never been more grateful to be proven wrong.

He blinked. "Sometimes I wonder. Come on, let's go." He started across the bridge.

"No, Nic, wait."

He glanced back and arched an eyebrow.

I took a deep breath as my universe rediscovered its center of gravity. "Thank you."

"You're welc—"

He gagged on the word when I hugged him.

He let me savor it for three seconds—just long enough for it to be awkward—before he shoved me away. "You're welcome," he repeated, "but don't *ever* hug me again."

I wasn't sure whether to laugh or cry, so I did both.

He rolled his eyes again. "Let's get out of here. I need a coffee."

"I'll buy," I teased, and followed him onto the bridge.

"Leaving so soon?"

Nic froze, every muscle in his body rigid.

I whipped around. Asia emerged from the trees on the shore and came to stand on the end of the bridge behind us. She posed under the light of the lamppost, hand on her hip like a femme fatale in a frame.

Nic refused to turn around. "You know I hate parties."

His tone was cold, easy, familiar, and I suddenly realized that I should be very afraid. "You two… know each other?"

"More than I'd like," Nic hissed.

"And not as much I'd hoped," Asia cackled at the same time. She strolled towards us with the ease of a cat who'd cornered its prey. "But we can make up for lost time. Won't you two join me? They're just about to serve dessert." She gestured across the lake at the party.

"Regrettably, Andromeda is an extremely busy woman, so we'll have to catch up later." Nic grabbed my hand and started to pull me across the bridge.

"Nic, don't be so cruel. I've waited *eight years* for you to accept my invitation—the least you could do is spare fifteen minutes." Asia flicked her fingers, and armed guards emerged from the trees behind her. Several more materialized at the far end of the bridge, cutting us off from both sides. There was nowhere to go but into the water.

I gripped Nic's hand as my throat closed in fear. *Oh God, no.*

Asia flashed a perfect smile. "Dr. Von Nieuwenhuyse, you're under arrest."

TO BE CONTINUED...

FIRST LIGHT

RED RAIN #5.5

RACHEL NEWHOUSE

I hated parties.

As a general rule, they involved too many people and too little productivity. State dinners were even worse, as the majority of the attendees had no business being there. The dregs of society tended to wash up at government events, floating in on the sponsorship of privileged friends. They would cling like mollusks to affluent attendees, muddying the waters for those of us who had actual work to accomplish.

That's the only reason I came to this particular government function. I had been presented with an award and was a keynote speaker, but the only thing I wanted to walk away with was more sponsors for my experiments.

On account of said award, I could have had anyone in the room I wanted, but most of them were not worth my time. Because of the sensitive nature of my work, I needed a very specific kind of patron.

Those in the upper echelons of society weren't worth the risk; they had everything to lose and nothing to gain. Those in the lower ranks didn't have the resources I needed. But the aspiring politicians in the middle—those were my primary targets. They had enough money to be useful to me, and they had everything to gain. An underappreciated director with a shot at a higher seat was willing to bend the rules if it meant winning valuable allies. If I found one who was disgruntled enough, they might even be willing to help me break the system entirely.

I spent the evening filtering the crowd, searching for the up-and-coming. I would introduce myself, allow them to flatter themselves a bit, and then sow a seed of hope—the mere suggestion that I could be useful to them. Then I would walk away, leaving them to simmer in their imagination for a while. By the time I returned, they were ready to sign.

It was a delicate process that involved balancing a dozen active leads simultaneously. I couldn't afford to get distracted—

which was why I was extremely annoyed when the daughter of Chairman Mong approached me.

Anyone else would have been beside themselves. As third in line to the General Secretary, Chairman Mong had earned the privilege of not talking to people. Instead, he spied out his prey from across the room and sent one of his lesser councilmen to make the arrangements.

His daughter, a chairwoman of some standing in her own right, also had the honor of being his carrier pigeon. She spent the evening watching his face for subtle nods and gestures. I knew this because she and I had inadvertently exchanged several glances.

As she strode towards me, her clicking stilettos heralding her approach, I realized that those glances may have been intentional on her part.

I decided to cut her off at the pass in hopes of keeping the intrusion brief. I met her halfway across the ballroom and offered my hand. "Madame Mong, I'm Dr. Nic."

She clasped my hand with a fearless grip. "Shi Min Tai," she offered.

I blinked. She'd skipped at least three phases of formal introduction and jumped straight to given names.

Well, that escalated quickly.

"Charmed," I said, and lightly pumped her hand. "Which do you prefer?"

"Excuse me?"

"If we are going on a first name basis, three given names seems excessive. Which do you prefer?"

She grinned, showing perfect teeth. "The boys in Washington call me Asia." She withdrew her hand from mine, slowly, her fingers brushing my palm. "But I prefer Min."

I hesitated, fully aware of the risks associated with that invitation.

She waited patiently.

I accepted the offer. "Pleasure to meet you, Min." In exchange, I offered her one of my rare smiles—the most valuable currency I had on me at the moment.

She seemed pleased with the sacrifice. "Congratulations on the award. From what I've heard, you deserve it."

"You seem to think so."

My prophetic insight stumped her, as it did with everyone. She arched one thin, penciled eyebrow. "I'm sorry?"

"Forgive me for noticing, but your father didn't send you over here."

She instinctively glanced back at him. Chairman Mong hadn't paid me any mind all evening, for which I was grateful. I was not interested in bargaining with him; he was one of the people I hoped would suffer when I succeeded.

No, Min had sought me out of her own volition—a fact I found extremely suspicious.

When she turned back to me, her dark eyes glinted like stars swallowed by a black hole. "You're a smart man, Nic."

"I wouldn't be worth your time if I wasn't." I shifted and glanced around the room. Several jealous—and prying—eyes were angled in our direction, no doubt wondering what wizardry I had pulled to secure Min's attention. Whatever she wanted, she'd better make it fast.

I turned back to her and spread my hands. "What can I do for you, Min?"

She devoured my subservience with a ravenous grin. "I want to sponsor your project."

"I'd be honored," I said, even though I wasn't. I did not like people who volunteered their money without first listening to my speech. That meant they had something to gain—something I hadn't sold them. "May I ask what interests you about my work?"

She opened her diamond-encrusted clutch and rifled through the contents. "The science speaks for itself, doesn't it?"

Of course it did—but not to people like Min. My project was, by design, deceptively mundane. I had developed a unique blend of plastic that was resistant to almost every acidic compound on the spectrum. The result had significant implications for the medical and industrial fields, but that was hardly the kind of advancement that concerned people of Min's status.

She withdrew a lipstick from her purse. "I think the science has other… uses, don't you?"

It did. That was the whole reason I developed it—because I ultimately intended to store something other than cleaning products in the canisters.

And that was exactly why I had to be very careful about who got involved.

I pretended to straighten my bowtie. "Is the Chairman interested in other applications?"

"Hardly." With a deft hand, she swiped a fresh layer of bloodred paint on her lips. "But I might be."

"'Might'?" I fought the urge to laugh. "As much as I love a good experiment, that is not a probability I want to test."

She clicked her lipstick case shut. "Not a man to take a risk, are we, Dr. Nic?"

The insult tickled my rage, and I realized I'd lost the upper hand in the conversation a long time ago. "I am quite comfortable taking risks," I snapped. "But only necessary ones."

"As am I. I hate an unnecessary mess." She dropped the lipstick in her purse and looked up at me. "But I can assure you this is a well-calculated risk."

Clearly, she was now trying to sell me on the deal, so I deferred the stage to her. "What are your terms?"

"I have some personal projects you may be able to help me with in the future." She looked up and met my eyes. "But in the meantime, I've looked at your portfolio. I know people who can fund everything on your list. I would be happy to introduce you."

I filtered her words through my mental translation program, trying to decode any pauses or inflections that might tell me what she was up to. If I said yes, I'd be dancing with the devil; her father could ruin me with a finger snap.

But if she meant what she said, I could have everything I wanted—and a clear shot at her father when I was ready to take it.

I held out my hand. "I expect my project to cost a great deal of money."

She took it with a smile. "Leave it to me."

AVAILABLE NOW!

WANT EXCLUSIVE BONUS SCENES?

Become a Patron and get access to **exclusive bonus scenes** for this book! This bonus content is not available anywhere else, and I post a new scene every month. Plus, you can get digital ARCs, signed paperbacks, collector's edition hardbacks, and merch, or read my WIP as I write it!

Become a Patron at:
patreon.com/rachelnewhouse

Or sign up for my newsletter and be the first to hear about new releases—plus get sneak peeks of upcoming books, cover art, and more!

Sign up at:
rachelnewhouse.com/subscribe

DID YOU LOVE THIS BOOK?

Please consider leaving a review on Amazon or Goodreads! It's one of the most important things you can do to support an indie author. Thank you!

HI FROM RACHEL

Rachel Newhouse is an author, wife, secretary, and Sunday school teacher from Kansas City, Missouri. Her obsessions are sci-fi, dystopian, and kid lit. When she's not writing, she's cooking Asian food, growing chilis that are too spicy to eat, and watching wildly age-inappropriate shows like *My Little Pony* and *Gravity Falls* with her husband, Joe. She also really likes glitter. You've been warned.

Connect with Rachel:
bio.site/rachelnewhouse